Plastic Vodka Bottle Sleepover

Plastic Vodka Bottle Sleepover

a novel

Mila Jaroniec

Published by Split Lip Press
333 Sinkler Road
Wyncote, PA 19095
www.splitlippress.com

ISBN: 978-0-9909035-8-1

Cover design by Jayme Cawthern
Back cover photo by Allison Good, Catcake Photography, *catcakephotography.com*

For MD

The kitchen is overrun with flies.

Last night when the air was cool I opened the balcony door to let some of it in, make the stagnant air in the room less so, but instead all that happened were the flies. Not the tiny innocent fruit flies that seem to come from nowhere but the beefy, demanding outdoor flies that zoom in like black torpedoes the minute you crack a window, swarming plague-like into the kitchen and enveloping it in a sharp metallic hum. When this happens I try to avoid the kitchen, but tonight I remember the vodka in the freezer and wade through the abrasive whirr of wings.

I find two. One is a large bottle of Sobieski that Mischa brought over weeks ago for my birthday, still untouched, and the other is the last sip of shitty lemon Smirnoff left over from a house party. The bottom shelf has a half-eaten strawberry and a small heap of broken glass. The strawberry has been there since I moved in but I have never thought to remove it, more interested instead in watching its progression of decay. Even now, little appears to have changed. It looks almost the same as it did last winter, its quilted red skin more shrunken and age-spotted but fairly taut and well preserved. I pick up the Sobieski and shut the freezer door.

An enormous fly collides with my hand as I reach for the cabinet above the sink, its prickly body vibrating against me like an electrified jellybean before speeding away. I wipe my hand on my jeans and stand up on tiptoe to reach the top shelf, feeling around for a clean glass. Eventually I hit upon an oversized coffee mug in the way back, the only one not lying with the graveyard of dishes in the sink, a heavy, hand-painted behemoth plastered in multicolored peace signs and Grateful Dead bears. I unscrew the bottle and tip it carefully into the mug.

I walk back into the bedroom, put the bottle on the floor next to my feet and sit down in front of my laptop, swallowing a chilly mouthful. Almost immediately I feel a powerful surge of heat rise up in my neck and cheeks, unfurl and spread throughout my limbs with the delicious warmth of morphine. A clock is ticking somewhere – tick-*tick* – probably in the closet, but I don't feel like digging for it. I turn on some music and try to tune it out. Somehow this makes the flies in the kitchen sound even louder. Tick-*tick*.

Maybe it's two clocks.

I flip open the screen and look up pictures of Courtney Love. Her trademark smear of scarlet lipstick pops up, along with a multitude of other familiar shots: the hard white jaws and silky pink dresses, the sad comic curve of her lips glazed over with a rotten film of sweetness and decay. A girl I knew in real life looked nothing like Courtney but still somehow resembled her in a way, the way she was all mouth, all wild speech and intensity, all sweat and bright veins running down her open legs. A girl no one knew all the way. A girl who could change people. Who changed me.

I scroll through the endless pages of dirty bleached hair, mesmerized, hundreds of half-burnt cigarettes stuck in various iterations of her gash-like mouth. Strong chins and protruding cheekbones, the vacant glacial blue of her eyes and the way her face appears to fold in on itself. You can see it in some pictures more than in others.

I put a hand to my own lips, which, unlike Courtney's, are not my best feature, small and strange like the lips on Venetian masks, the porcelain kind with graphic eyes and sculpted noses, miniature bow lips pert and unyielding below the philtrum, facial features descending in order of size. Until recently I used to convince myself that my lips could also be full and commanding if I put in the extra work, routinely planting myself in front of the bathroom mirror with a stick of lip liner for hours, rimming my pouted mouth in tenuous strokes of dark red slightly wider than normal. Of course I could never get it perfectly even, and when the lipstick wore off the liner bled out too, feathering and seeping past the outer edges into a fuzzy scarlet halo.

Sometimes when you look in the mirror you see a stranger in the place you used to be, especially if you fixate too long on one particular point, a single pore or a stray hair on your chin. It's the same thing that happens when you say a word twenty times in a row, over and over until you don't know the meaning of it anymore. Something gets lost between the worlds. You lose all points of reference, the word becomes all sound – *why are you making that sound?* – and for that moment your whole working concept of meaning gets all tilt-shift, hollow space after a thing scraped out that only vaguely bears its shape, dark water where your feet can't touch the bottom. Look at yourself a while longer and your features melt together, touch and your fingers fall through the fleshy surface straight into the skull cavities, like pushing apart the muscle of an overcooked fish.

I finish the vodka and shut my laptop. There's a good third of the bottle left but it'll have to get warm. The thought of going back into the fly-infested kitchen makes my stomach turn. A copy of *The Diving Bell and the Butterfly* I'd borrowed from Mischa and never read is sitting on the desk next to me. I pick it up and flip through the pages. The butterfly's wings on the cover are tinged a dark moody red. Apparently the author composed the book solely by blinking his left eyelid, the only part of him that remained functional after a massive stroke. As far as I know the doctors sewed up the right eyelid, probably because it wasn't able to move on its own and the eye got dry all the time. Or maybe they just got tired of watching it loll around pointlessly. Which was equally possible. I don't think you get to be a doctor without a minuscule sadistic streak.

An angry fizz breaks the silence and I look out to see the flies committing suicide against the kitchen lamp, their singed bodies sparking with a crackle before dropping into a pile on the floor. I sketch a fly outline on the cover in black Sharpie.

I open the laptop back up and create a second tab, taking one last look at Courtney's abrasive sadness before logging into Orbitz.com.

What am I doing in this goddamn airport?

That was the first of many unanswerable questions. It didn't hit me until after the first part, the adrenaline-rush part, the *holy shit we're going on an adventure* part, after I fed my seam-splitting purse and spiky wedge heels into the conveyor belt X-ray thing and walked through the state-of-the-art weapon detector, appeared again on the other end and sat down on the metal bench to put my shoes back on and collect myself, only then did the reality of the present moment register and I started to really think about what I was doing. The initial feeling of crazy confidence, that momentary surge of action and energy and the feeling that I was DOING SOMETHING and that something was about to HAPPEN had slowly degenerated into a creeping sense of horror and despair.

I looked back out onto the security line, the zoo of obstacles and general confusion I was now on the other side of. A pool of heavily made-up American women was thickening around an old man planted in front of the belt. He was untying his shoes slowly, as if removing a sleeping lover's. Time seemed to gel around him. Behind him the women started to roll their eyes and sigh dramatically, wilting off to one side in an exaggerated contrapposto. If this were Poland, I thought, someone would have helped him take off those damn shoes by now. People are in your face a lot more in Poland. Though in situations like this it's not always a bad thing.

What if I just walked back out? I wondered how I would feel about myself then. There was something very carefree and windblown about it, something very romantic and nouveau riche about the idea of dropping $300 on a spontaneous plane ticket only to change your mind at the last minute and breeze right back through the gate to emotional safety. Carrie does something similar in an episode of *Sex and the City* but I remember her being a lot more conflicted about it, she rents a car to surprise her on-a-break writer boyfriend but only makes it two meters out of the garage before realizing it's a terrible idea. In light of this, what I was doing seemed infinitely worse. At least Carrie had a boyfriend to ambush.

I pondered this, but decided to stay put. Even if something is painfully stupid, I've always been the type to see it through to the very end. Just to see what happens, if nothing else.

It all seemed like a great idea last night, when I was drunk out of my head. Lots of things seem like great ideas when you're drunk out of your head, but sometimes you get a particularly great idea that demands immediate action, and if you're really down in it you actually go and do something before your self-preservation instinct kicks in and your brain gets a chance to either sober up or shut down. Sort of like playing roulette with your future, if getting drunk is loading all but one chamber.

And I'm pretty sure the only reason people drink like this, to the point where the next move is a toss up – especially people who deal with the side effects of drinking sort of mournfully, like I do – the only reason we drink like this is to get down into the wells of ourselves and sift through the piles of emotional refuse buried there. There's always something just out of mental reach, some crucial understanding of ourselves we can't arrive at in our fully competent, conscious states that only becomes accessible with a little help, alcohol or religion or LSD. With us, the little bit of raw soul is stuck under a hard layer of acrylic and alcohol is the acetone soak.

So there I was, drunk out of my head for the thousandth time, trying to get to a place where things would feel less on top of me and I could start to peel them apart and make sense of them, but instead I began to sink into the realization of how much I missed Sloan, how life without her was kind of bullshit, just a half life really, artificial and with no real intensity, punctuated by spooky thoughts of how I was going to die alone, last words uttered to an empty room or my deathbed nurse or someone else who didn't care I was dying, and armed with these new clarities I dove straight into my purse, dug my credit card out of the tobacco-lined bottom and, squinting liquidly into the glow of my laptop, slowly and carefully tapped the row of numbers into Orbitz.com. New York to Austin December 28th, the day before her birthday. Austin to New York December 30th, in case things went well or badly. When the confirmation page popped up I shut the laptop, feeling satisfied and excited that something was about to HAPPEN, and passed out on top of it.

That was last night, and this morning I woke up very hazy and fluid and out of my head, definitely still drunk but pleasantly loose, the kind of loose when you wake up in sleep-stale clothes wearing last night's smile and you think you can ride out the residual high and still have a good day because the hangover hasn't hit you yet, and won't until sometime in the afternoon, when the sickness comes on and you start to feel paralyzed, but for now you're still out on your own stretch of sunrise and yep, you bought a plane ticket last night because the impulse control part of your brain was the first thing to go when you started in on the vodka, because diluting your blood made the whisper inside it a full-bodied hum, because Just How Fucking Bad you missed her finally filtered in from the back of your consciousness to the hard gleaming forefront, and now here you are in the middle of the goddamn airport with nothing but a credit card, two pairs of underwear and an unread copy of *Hopscotch* at the bottom of your shitty purse, feeling increasingly ill and horrified at the Reality and Consequences of what you're about to do barreling into you head-on.

I get my shoes on and head in the direction of the gate. B6. If nothing else I could think of it as a vacation. Austin wasn't the most exciting, but it was still a new city. Even if I ended up accomplishing nothing I would be doing so in the best place, a place where I knew no one and nothing was expected. I could float around the hotel pool. Go for a half-assed run in the tiny exercise room. Wander around and look at things, examine the architecture, loiter on street corners without having to worry about whose way I was in, approach things in that extrasensitive way you approach them when they're familiar things in an unfamiliar place you've paid good money to be in. I could pick up beautiful strangers, feeling safe in the knowledge I'd never see them again. I could smoke, relax, do nothing. Think of this as a mini meditation retreat. If nothing else.

But I couldn't think like that. I could think about what to do if things went badly when they actually started to go that way, but right now I had to come up with what to say to Sloan. Which at this point was still nothing.

I considered my options. I could take a cab downtown and ask her to meet me in a bar. Or wait somewhere close to her work. Or just show up at her apartment, by far the worst possibility but arguably the most effective. I pictured snippets of every scenario, each one more horrifying than the last. I remembered her saying there was a gate to her complex you had to unlock with a code before you could go through it. My original plan of waiting outside her door died a quick death.

I realized with a mounting paranoia that her girlfriend would probably be there. Of course she would be. It was almost Sloan's birthday. What kind of girlfriend would she be if she weren't at her apartment a night early, flitting around the kitchen in her lacy thong or boy shorts or whatever ass-accentuating underwear she wore, constructing a celebratory dinner for the woman I loved and making everything perfect? I wondered if that was still something people in love did, spent hours in the kitchen making dinners for each other, waiting with hopeful anticipation for the reaction to the first bite, or if at a certain point in the relationship you simply switched to takeout.

Or maybe this girl cooked naked. Maybe Sloan loved being cooked naked for. Maybe that's where she and I fucked up, cooking naked being something I'd never done. Or maybe she was one of those food fetish types, seducing Sloan with gourmet meals placed in various sexy contexts. I pictured Sloan coming home from work exhausted, requisite cigarette tucked in the corner of her mouth, going to toss her blazer on the kitchen table only to be surprised by a nude woman wearing a medium-rare filet for a merkin and whorls of sautéed onions around her nipples. I felt a stab of jealousy at the possibility of this random girl being better than me at something I'd never even thought of doing. I was just as capable of looping onions around my nipples. Fuck her.

I considered this, situating myself in a chair by the window and pulling *Hopscotch* from my purse. Should I take my chances with that? Just how crazy would it make me seem?

Probably not too crazy, given what Sloan used to consider romantic. If she still had any sense of her former self she would interpret what I was doing as the Breakneck Pivotal Thing, the thing that happens in movies when the main character realizes they've been hazy-eyed about their true love the entire time, and in textbook impractical fashion they do something big and wild and soul-baring that makes the neglected person cry tears of adoration and forgiveness and open their arms to them once more. The Breakneck Pivotal Thing is never done in something shitty and small like an email. In order for it to be genuine, the heart has to cover some physical ground.

Hopscotch. It was substantially heavy. I balance it on my knee and flip through the translucent pages, wispy like the ones in those New Testament Bibles militant Christians hand out on college campuses, smiling eagerly at the kids who actually accept, unwise to the fact that they've just supplied them with a fantastic amount of rolling papers. Sloan had given it to me before a visit to my mom's one spring.

"The perfect airport book," she said, placing it in my hands. "You'll see why."

Sloan had a thing for airports. I imagined it was sort of like the thing business-cum-family men had for bathrooms, a place where you're not expected to do anything but sit there and people generally leave you alone. But Sloan loved to watch the people. The myriad implications of people in transition made her feel happy to be alive, gave her that crucial jolt to the nervous system that only comes from a certain ecstatic curiosity not found in everyday life. Transition, journey, change, the idea of people with lives of varying stability picking up and going somewhere for some reason, or no reason, or something that might turn out to be nothing all gave her hope, hope with a capital H, the assurance that where you are isn't where you'll be forever if you don't want it to be, that even when you have nothing moving the one thing you can always do is move. She liked to create blueprints for where everyone was going, invent stories for them, superimpose narratives on their lives. Speculating on who would be there to pick them up from the airport, whether they'd be greeted with a hug or kiss or bitchslap or handshake, whether there would be someone on the other side holding up a Welcome Home sign or one with their first and last names awkwardly penned, whether anyone would pick them up at all. Whether they'd just descend the escalator to ground transportation with their one small carry-on, pass through the sliding doors alone to the taxi stand in the soft and empty night.

I flip all the way back to the inscription. Sloan inscribed all the books she gave as gifts in the back pages rather than the front. It was more personal, she said, because it gave the recipient something more to look for, all the way in the back where no one thinks to look, a closing message for the reader after the author's delivered theirs. I never used to check the backs of books for inscriptions but I started to after Sloan, in books I found in free boxes around the city or bought in used bookstores. I rarely find anything back there besides old receipts and half-finished shopping lists, but I still check every time.

The inscription read:

> *For La Maga, the one I always searched for, but never hoped to find. I hope this book does to you what it did to me.*
>
> *Oliveira*

From what I'd gathered from Sloan's synopsis, Oliveira is a writer in Paris on the verge of existential collapse, grappling with the meaning of things and having a hard time with the concept of meaning in general, when suddenly this beautiful, strange, unhinged-in-the-best-ways woman called La Maga crashes into his life, and with her everlasting cigarette and charmingly erratic behavior gives him rigor mortis of the heart.

Or something like that. I'd never actually read it. There was a small part of me that felt a paralyzing fear about the books Sloan deemed life-changing, as if I would find something in them I didn't really want to know, some vital and crippling fact about her that she knew, and the author knew. Something I needed to take my time discovering, or not discover at all. Even the times we were uncomfortably close and still wanted to get closer I knew there was something about her I wasn't ready to see, something in her fabric that was too tight-woven for me to tease apart myself, a deep central thing I felt unequipped to understand and desperately wanted to avoid. I spent a long time trying to work out what that exact thing was but gave up trying once it wasn't my problem anymore.

I wonder if that's as much a part of loving someone as wanting to find out everything about them, deliberately leaving something untouched. It feels almost disrespectful, in a way, wanting to know everything, that strange desire to get down under someone and shine a flashlight through their insides, but this one thing, not wanting to approach it out of fear or reverence or just plain being Not Ready, realizing there's a part of this person, this rolling ocean of virgin soul you're not quite built to handle –

How exactly are you supposed to make sense of a person, place them neatly in a schema, knowing there's something beneath their surface you shouldn't be clawing at, the half-open latch of Pandora's box, that sparkling dangerous thing breathing under the veil until you're brave enough to go under or they pull it off themselves?

"You can't keep doing this to yourself," Mischa said over matching lines of crushed Xanax a few days prior. "You weren't even happy with her. And anyway, how long has it been?"

She was hunched over a Rick Moody hardback at the rickety table, rolling a pint glass over the pills to flatten them into a fine dust. She was trying to make me see, through the wisdom afforded by her own broken heart, how ridiculous I was being by trying to scavenge anything from the ruin of Us. Sloan and I had been apart for over a year and I was still acting like someone with a damaged hippocampus, refusing to remember why we broke up to begin with, focusing on the Great Cosmic Meaning I had invented rather than accepting that it was simply, unceremoniously over. Things are, and then they are not.

"How can you just not see that?"

Vision problems.

I had gone straight to Mischa's that night after work, West Village to Crown Heights with an entire bag of shit from Whole Foods. Armed with fancy cheese, a bottle of whiskey and a decent supply of pharmaceuticals from Leigh, I traipsed the twelve blocks from the subway to her building, let myself in with the spare key and climbed the four flights of stairs to her newly emptied apartment. Our friendship had devolved into the sad sort of sexless marriage, with one partner losing their grip on everything and splintering into pieces while the other continues to pretend like nothing's wrong. Me banging through the door with groceries and toilet paper, her sunk listlessly in the couch. The door sucked shut behind me.

"Mischa?"

Silence. A pale yellow light shone from the depths of the living room. My heart convulsed. What if she…? No, she hadn't. No way. I walked deeper into the room and found her curled up on the couch in a fetal position, the sharp points of her bones poking up through her shirt as if they were trying to escape her body.

I froze, waiting the obligatory two seconds to see her ribcage rise and fall, the same thing I used to do with my grandma when I came back from school and she'd been in bed all day, home alone. When I called her name and heard nothing I would run up to her bedroom and hover in the doorway, heart pounding, and look.

Sometimes her head would be thrown back on the pillow, mouth open and still, but each time I waited those two seconds until I saw the soft shift. Mischa's ribcage swelled and I lowered the bag to the floor with a heavy exhale, tiptoed over and knelt down next to her. I smoothed the wild curls off her face and pressed my lips to her forehead. She opened a sleepy eye.

"Hi. I brought treats."

She gave me a shaky smile and lifted herself into a sitting position.

"Great," she said. "I'm starving."

Within forty minutes Mischa consumed three mini cheesecakes, two cups of miso soup, several curlicued hunks of peanut butter, a heaping bowl of pesto spaghetti, the olive oil pooled in a slick green well at the bottom, and several pieces of day-old sushi. After a short break she laid into half a block of Irish cheddar, a handful of apple slices, and the debris of stale potato chips that had been on the living room floor for days. She licked the yellow crumbs off her fingers, dabbing at the greasy foil inside the bag to pick up more. If it were anyone else it would've been disgusting, but I was glad she was eating. Since Krista left she hadn't eaten at all.

When she was done with the chips she brushed the bag to the floor and folded herself back into the couch, the faded cushions imprinted with the outline of her shape. She pulled an ugly baby blanket up to her face and burrowed into it. Her voice came out frail from within the folds of fabric.

"Do you think she'll come back?"

"I don't know," I said. "Maybe."

"Maybe, you think so?"

"I don't know. Does it matter?"

She went quiet. I reached over and pulled the blanket, wet with fresh tears, off her face. I felt the full magnitude of my protectiveness of her then, like she was made of the most fragile material and it was my sacred duty to keep her safe. Not only was it my job to keep her out of harm's way, but for the rest of my life I'd have to work to make her better, produce some sort of blueprint for repairing her broken heart.

On the other hand, fuck. If strong, sensible Mischa was powerless against heartbreak, there wasn't a whole lot to be said for anyone else. This was a case of the blind leading the sleeping. But I would try my best.

I extracted the baggie of pills from my pocket.

"Misch," I said. "Here."

She sucked up a line and leaned back in the chair.

"I'm telling you, it's never going to work. You were miserable before and you're miserable now. She's not even here and she's making you miserable. That's a hell of an accomplishment. And anyway, you broke up with her."

"You say that like it means something."

"Doesn't it?"

I sighed and looked down at my phone. Sloan was in there, flashes of texts flooding in one by one, but inside me nothing moved. We were supposed to be being Friends. Friends meant asking how each other's day was going, phone calls during long walks or drives to stave off boredom, feigning interest in the painfully innocuous day-to-day we cautiously shared. Texting each other photos of cheeky sandwich boards outside of bars. She never mentioned her girlfriend more than she had to. Friends meant no more screaming fights, no more transcendental sex, no more getting piss drunk and making out with strangers and no more butcher blocks hurled against the wall. We were keeping each other at a safe distance and it was a good thing, it was the healthy thing to do, but even with all these new and pure intentions something about us felt fake, put on, like a skin graft. Like stretching something fresh bred in a Petri dish over the frayed hole of a dead thing in full bloom of decay. I would have happily taken an errant knife sailing past my head, anything that meant there was a modicum of emotion left. Anything that wasn't this.

I looked at Mischa, busy steamrollering a second set of pills under the plastic baggie. A clump of dark curls had fallen out of her hair tie and was hanging in her face, obscuring her work. I stifled a laugh.

"What?"

"Nothing. It's just…we're 25."

"So? It takes faster this way."

Within twenty minutes she was out cold, but I wasn't. I kicked the blanket off my overheated legs, careful not to disturb her half. She let out a deep sigh and wrapped an arm around my waist, molding her body to my back. I felt her breath against my neck and shivered.

"I love you," she murmured.

I had an instinct to move away but instead I moved closer and draped my forearm over hers, curling my legs to cup her knees pressed into the backs of mine. Her sleep-heavy arm settled in the hollow between ribs and hip and I slowed my breath to match her rhythm, eventually going dark to the rise and fall of our chests, bones touching bones.

Sloan lifted my arm up and slid hers underneath it, draping it over my waist. She hugged me tighter to her, closing off the space between us. The breeze blowing in through the open windows made the frayed curtains undulate like gauzy jellyfish. I felt goosebumps cropping up on my skin but I didn't reach for the blanket, afraid to disturb the delicate balance of our bodies. I knew if I moved it would be impossible to recreate the positioning, and I could have stayed in that cozy purgatory forever.

Supertrust, she called it, this thing we were doing that normal people refer to as spooning. Spooning sounded vulgar, she said, and also that when she was being intimate she didn't want to be thinking about silverware. Supertrust, on the other hand, was the only word in which you could accurately describe this level of closeness. I always pictured Supertrust as some kind of pacifist comic book hero, but I let her have it. Usually she insisted on being completely naked, but after I ended up with pneumonia from countless nights of having to sleep pushed up against the brick wall with nothing but a layer of skin for protection, she stopped taking personally my desire to wear clothes to bed.

"So where are we going to go after graduation?" She pressed herself in closer, tracing circles around each vertebra. "LA? New York?" She listed some other cities. Sloan was about to graduate herself and wanted desperately to move, escape the shitty small town we were living in and start a new life with me somewhere else, doing something else. Obviously she could see further in front of her than I could, being a year ahead, and also the type who knew how to make plans, and I told her so. I didn't know where to go next, what the next move that made sense was. The deeper I went in my philosophy major the more strongly I was realizing two very depressing, important things: one, that there was no way I could build a life on answering unanswerable questions, and two, that I didn't have a strong inclination toward anything else. When I was younger I had vaguely envisioned myself a writer, but that idea got poisoned out of me at an early age. Something Practical was the condition under which my mother allowed me to go to college, and I tacked philosophy onto a pre-med major under the argument that it helped you get into med school (it doesn't) because she wouldn't let me just have the first. *Musimy jakoś żyć, czy istniejemy czy nie*, she said, and I didn't argue. We have to make a living somehow, whether we exist or not.

"You can't work in a sex shop forever," Sloan continued, folding a hand over my hipbone. "You're better than that. We're better than that."

Except the only reason we had any money to spend was because I did work in a sex shop. Why she disapproved of it so much was a mystery to me. For a textbook sex maniac she was shockingly prude. Sex for Sloan only had a place in the dark, where you couldn't see what you were doing. In the dark sex was beautiful and holy. You could reduce yourself to your individual parts and become all cunt, all hands and mouth and tidal blood pound, separate orbits of cellular electricity. Multisected. But in the daylight that purity became diminished, broken down by vision and speech on contact. Apparently this also applied to the discussion of sex with strangers.

"You know that, don't you?" Fingers up my spine. "How do you even stand the way they look at you?"

"At least it's more interesting than making fucking sandwiches."

It wasn't like she was the goddamned master of operations at the campus café. Every other week they were threatening to fire her for a plethora of bullshit reasons like not wearing a hairnet (Sloan in a hairnet!) or being constantly late or taking too many cigarette breaks. Beyond that, I didn't see how stuffing meatballs into a bread cylinder was so much more respectable than selling vibrators and condoms when both had to do with survival, but she was impossible to convince.

I had found Eden during my first week of college, wandering up the street of the arts district. "Arts district," a term used loosely. The whole thing spanned a total of five blocks maximum, a noble-faced crumbling sprawl where the city dumped the only places that didn't cater to the football-and-family-values crowd, a handful of overcrowded gay bars interspersed throughout rows of shops that sold stuff, just stuff. Lots of upscale motel art and things people buy when they already have their made-to-look-antique glassware and the only thing missing is a taxidermied peacock, or a mortar and pestle to smash their organic avocados in.

The window display announced a fetish shop. A chipped girl mannequin, in all her PVC-wrapped glory, held a similarly chipped boy mannequin loosely on a leash with her stiff-fingered hand. A cherry red ball gag hung from a dusty leather strap around his mouth. Miscellaneous accoutrements were placed around them for balance, riding crops, shrink-wrapped magazines with pony girls on the cover, black suede roses mounted on wire stems bunched inside a clear glass vase. A sun-bleached Now Hiring sign was taped to the front door.

I went in.

Where I grew up we had only one sex shop, on the side street of a strip mall behind the Starbucks that used to be Brady's Café, headed up by a crew of sweat-pantsed women with penciled eyebrows who looked like they had no idea how they got there and really just wanted to go home. They were definitely not in the mood for questions, especially not about what kind of lube went best with what dildo material. *Look,* their faces told the feather-haired housewives, *Just use Crisco if you're going to be cheap about it. Like I give a fuck.*

But this place wasn't like that. It had all kinds of incredible implements I'd never seen before, much less thought about using in the context of another human body. Coils of rope in all the colors of the rainbow sat atop one another in a finger-smudged case. Handcuffs in every shade and finish of leather lined the wall behind the counter, studded, plain, heavy duty, rhinestone, not a pair of modest silk ties in the mix. An array of speculums, plastic and metal, that ranged in order of openness from is-it-in-yet to OB/GYN from hell. An entire case devoted solely to nipple clamps. The smoky scent of leather settled over everything like a wet cloud. A few solitary gray men shuffled quietly through the porn section in the back.

"Can I help you?" A hoarse voice broke the silence.

I turned in its direction to find a middle-aged man, fat beyond belief, crammed into a tiny chair behind a desk to the left of the door. His frizzy salt and pepper hair was wild and hung down to his shoulders. He wore smudged bifocals and there were about nine pens stuffed into his breast pocket. He heaved himself out of the chair and leaned against the counter, where his fingers, coated with a fine layer of Cheeto dust, imprinted orange whorls on the glass.

"Yes, I'd like to fill out an application." I pointed to the sign.

"Do you have any experience?"

Did he mean retail experience? Or fetish store experience? Or both? It didn't matter, because I had neither.

"Yes," I said. "I've worked retail before."

"Have you worked in a place like this before?"

"No, but I've read about this kind of stuff. And I'm a fast learner."

"Really?" He shifted his weight from one foot to the other. "What have you read?"

Fuck. I thought about all the books I had archived in my wish list in case some extra funds ever came along, Sacher-Masoch and de Sade and all the others no bookstore back home ever carried. They came recommended by the back pages of Inga's copy of *Bohemian Manifesto,* which she'd taken off the shelf and tossed to me during my first visit to her apartment, before she married my brother and the two of us still got along. Inga had an aggressive mass of curly black hair that she saw no point in brushing and outfitted her sinewy, wax-colored body in a color palette ranging from charcoal to mildew, crafted crumbly vegan quiches and refused to tweeze her eyebrows. Naturally, twelve-year-old me thought her more qualified than anyone to be the purveyor of truths contained in a book called *Bohemian Manifesto.* A cliché choice for a personal bible, I felt comforted nonetheless by the degrees of liberating strangeness that were possible, were celebrated, in collective human life. The fact that Gérard de Nerval used to take his pet lobster on walks around Paris in a three-piece suit (de Nerval, not the lobster), Verlaine so crazy sick with love he used the gun he was supposed to kill himself with to blow a hole in Rimbaud's hand, the fact that if you were an artist it was understood and expected that you would change your name.

"*The Story of O,*" I lied. "And some de Sade. *Justine, Philosophy in the Bedroom...*" I ticked off the first few titles from my list.

"And what did you think of them?"

Jesus, what kind of interview was this? I hadn't even filled out an application and already he was asking me more about my literary observations than any English teacher ever had. The absurdity of what I was doing got to me then, standing around in the faded afternoon light of a Midwestern sex shop with my too-long hair and too-clear complexion, an affront to the knowledge I didn't have. He probably had to deal with clueless college kids coming through every day, asking for a job he knew they couldn't handle and didn't really want. I pictured a blonde ex-volleyball player with a White Strips smile nervously demonstrating how to fashion a gimp mask over a mannequin head.

"They were visionary," I said. "They overstepped culturally accepted sexual boundaries, and by so doing called them into question, spurring a deeper exploration of sexual and societal values in general."

Any English teacher would have given me an A for that response.

He nodded.

"Well, here's an application," he said, bending down to the squeaky filing cabinet and extracting a thick piece of paper. "Fill this out and bring it back tomorrow if you can, and then we'll talk."

I took the paper from him, feeling like I'd won something.

"And try to read one or two of those books you mentioned. I think you'd really enjoy them."

I don't remember much about you but I remember I used to make you draw me dinosaurs when I was a kid. I'd go up to your room with a notebook and pencil and say dinozaura, prosze – dinosaur, please – and tug on your sleeve and pout until you stopped doing whatever you were doing and obliged. Nag Champa smoke, Pink Floyd on the record player.

The funny thing is it didn't matter to me what you drew – I remember really liking the T-Rex and having no patience for the triceratops – but usually kids are particular and beyond that I had no preference. I just liked seeing you form the lines. And whatever you made I believed in. There were no live dinosaurs to use as a point of reference so that was enough to convince me you couldn't be wrong.

Occasionally your room contained Leah. I think she was your girlfriend at one point because I remember her wearing your t-shirts and I found a picture of the two of you buried in the drawer when I was going through it, junior prom, your shoulder-length hair and sloping eyebrows topping off a cheap rented suit, her sugar-blonde curls and shellacked crimson smile framing columns of perfect white teeth. Leah did ballet and ate dry spaghetti straight out of the box. The twigs emitted a sinister snap between the teeth. She rolled her eyes and sighed whenever I came in with the notebook, which in retrospect I understand, being seventeen and having the house to yourself and then being thwarted by a three-year-old, but the action of that. Being pushed out of your home by a stranger.

I saw her that week, actually, at the Starbucks that used to be Brady's Café. Same hair, same lips, same town. It looked like she cooked her spaghetti now. I was no longer three so she didn't know me, and I said nothing because I never knew her.

Leigh and I only fuck on weekdays.

I knock and she opens the door for me. Her place is cheerful for a basement apartment, the likes of which are depressing on principle, the scattered odds and ends bathed in afternoon sun imparting the sort of air that trendy home decorating magazines might describe as "whimsy." It probably looks different at night, but I've never been here at night. She and Stacy still live together and it's a definite unwritten rule that even after you transition from lovers to roommates, at-home hours are off limits.

Leigh kisses me on the cheek. I smile at her and walk in, sit down on the couch and cross my legs. Something about her always makes me want to fold into myself, become as small as my body will go. She asks if I want a drink. I do, but I say no. The only thing worse than fucking someone you shouldn't in a place you're not supposed to be is fucking with your consciousness beforehand. Every time she invites me over I know hers is the last place she wants me to be, and I wonder sometimes if that's why I go.

I've tried to figure out what she smells like before and I can't. To me it's always been laundry and shampoo, something clean and unfussy and deceptively plain, which is what she is. It blends with my own scent after we fuck, on our clothes and the pillows, when I try to soak up as much of her as I can before she disentangles herself and makes me leave for the night. Laundry and shampoo mixed with vanilla and smoke. She could also be wearing an ironic signature blend of laundry and shampoo, from one of those artisanal perfume houses that charge you an arm and a first born to smell like Fresh Lobster or Manhole, but she's never struck me as the type that would go out of her way to be ironic. I give up thinking about it and ask her what she smells like.

Just laundry and shampoo, she says.

She fucks me patiently, consistently, like she always does. She's a very thorough person but the idea of that has always felt jarring, the idea of people being thorough in bed, when that's the word you use to describe them, *thorough*. It makes me think of Cara, my middle school biology lab partner who would rip up the poster and make us start over if she thought we had sloppy-looking mitochondria. I wonder if she ended up a molecular biologist like she wanted. If she's seeing anyone, and if she isn't, if she's just as thorough.

I feel Leigh speed up and glance at the clock. It's 3:30. Her roommate will be home soon and I can tell she wants me to hurry. I'm splayed out in all directions and I'm losing my balance – the couch has no arms and there's the glass coffee table – so I throw my arms open and hold onto nothing as I turn it all off and make myself finish.

When I step back out into the clear afternoon I vow never to see her again, but I don't think I believe myself.

I was a virgin at the time. A virgin to girls, even though it's tacky to say that. I had a boyfriend but it didn't make much difference, we were nineteen and both dating each other to have something to do. He was a philosophy major too. His apartment was this rundown basement shithole in the half-bad part of town, bad enough to make you scared walking around at night but not quite bad enough to make you move back in with your parents or get a place on campus with a friend from high school, that sort of thing. I'd seen him in the library a few times before but we didn't talk then, he just kept glancing at me in the same furtive way the other boys did. I noticed him specifically because he looked like an odd steampunk version of Lord Byron, all grommets and slim hands and black cloves and long hair. Attractive in his own right, with a particular artery of strangeness I'd seen before in other sad boys but couldn't quite read. I fell in love with him, I think, because he understood about Sartre and salvia and all the things a girl fresh out of a sheltered home craves.

I was smoking outside a coffeehouse before finals when I saw her walking up the street. I knew the walk, that confrontational forward roll. As she approached I recognized her as the quiet girl from Ethics, the one who sat right in front and always looked like she'd just swallowed something sour. She stopped in front of me and flipped open a pack of Marlboro Reds.

"Got a light?" She reached into the pack, which was empty. "Actually, got a spare?"

"Sure."

I handed her a Newport and a packet of matches. She put the cigarette in her mouth and struck one, dropping her empty pack on the sidewalk.

I examined her out of the corner of my eye. She smoked like she got paid to do it, great lush inhales that seemed to descend right into the pit of her being. Spiky hair and charcoal liner, both messy on purpose, tight plaid shirt, skater shoes from the mall. She was short and muscular, but meaty, as if she used to be an athlete at one point but stuck to the meal plan long after she stopped training, the hard muscle disappearing under a languorous layer of fat. A sludgy pair of Doc Martens amplified the fact that she walked like a tank. She looked like a kid who'd raided her brother's closet and mother's vanity, stage makeup and army boots. There was a light smattering of freckles over her serious, milk thistle face.

Then there were her hands. Elegant, streamlined hands are the ones I usually go for, with long tapered fingers that can manipulate a piano or reach deep inside of me, but hers were not built that way. They were small and squat, thick-knuckled, with short stubby fingers that looked like they used to be longer but someone had broken them and shaved the tips off a third of the way through. Action hands. Hands made to push and punch and slap and grab. Hands that marked their territory, didn't trail off somewhere in the middle of the night because they got restless, never curved into two big question marks when held a certain way. Not poetry hands. Sure and solid and decidedly on top of whatever they laid themselves on.

I wondered what this girl thought of herself, what she thought about when choosing her clothes in the morning. I needed to understand the significance of the too-small shirt. Her bra made her tits double. Not like she was trying to be sexy, but like she bought bras that were too small on purpose because she didn't want to acknowledge her real cup size. I was sure the last time they both fit properly was in middle school. It was obvious she cared what people thought but in a very specific way, like the idea of herself she was trying to project only became clear in a certain frame of mind.

Or maybe not. Maybe there was no message at all, considering my tendency to read too deep into things.

"I gotta go," she said, flicking her half-smoked cigarette into the potted plant. "Thanks for the smoke. See you in class."

But I ended up seeing her that night. I had planned on doing more studying at home, but after so many hours of Kantian ethics I realized with a crowding hopelessness the only thing that could further my philosophical advances at that point was vodka. As I reached my apartment building I briefly considered going upstairs to change before grabbing a drink, but I doubted anyone in a basement bar on a Tuesday would care about my ripped hoodie or the vicious tangle of hair I affectionately called a topknot. Or my age. I swung open the door.

The spiky hair was sitting at the bar a few feet away from me. She was alone, as far as I could tell, bent intently over a glass with her cell phone up beside it, the way people do when they're out alone and want to look preoccupied.

"Hey," I said, easing onto a stool. "I didn't know you came here."

"I don't."

"Oh."

"Well, sometimes. The best thing about this place," she said, pulling a fresh pack of Marlboros out of her pocket, "is that you can smoke in it."

She flipped it open and extracted a cigarette with her teeth. I noticed her suck in her stomach a little and sit up straighter.

"Are you on your way home?"

"Sort of," I said. "I live upstairs."

"Oh."

"So what'd you do last weekend?" It was a lame question but this was painfully awkward. Typical pretentious philosophy type with too much to say and not enough to say it with, like so many of my classmates. Or my boyfriend. Or maybe she just thought I was boring. Either way.

Silence for a minute.

"Not much. Just fucked some girl in the bathroom on Saturday." She jerked her head toward the hall, where the bathroom was emitting its customary stench of piss and spilled beer. "You?"

"Not much. Just hung out with my boyfriend."

She took a deep drag of her cigarette, exhaled loudly and squished it into a powdery pulp in the ashtray.

"Okay. First one's on me."

Six vodka gimlets later, she started talking. There's usually a pretty small range of things people open up about when they're either drunk or getting there: their childhoods, dreams in various stages of fulfillment, and sex. Accordingly, I learned that Sloan had had an okay childhood, humble plans for the future, and tons of sex.

"Seriously," she said, tilting sideways on her stool. "You can try to get to know someone all you want, but you only really get to know them in bed."

"Yeah? How's that?"

"Think about it. People have all sorts of walls up when they talk to you. All sorts of mental blocks. But when they're under you, they don't have any armor. They're deconstructed. They're yours." She plucked out the forgotten cigarette smoldering in my fingers. "Ever fucked a girl before?"

"Once. In high school. She had fake nails." I winced at the memory.

"So you haven't. What's your boyfriend like?"

"I don't know. What they're normally like. Why, are you familiar?"

"Nope." She grinned. "Do you like it?"

"I guess. Sex is sex."

"Where is he tonight?"

She swiveled to face me. I became suddenly conscious of the heat in my cheeks, the smallness of my body in the gigantic black hoodie.

"Come on," she said, tugging my sleeve. "Let's go somewhere else."

She lived in the tiny attic room of a three-story house, what was essentially a wooden cube with a low slanted ceiling, with leaning bookcases and scattered ashtrays and a sunken mattress in the middle of the floor. I had never been undressed before, not really. I always liked to keep at least one article of clothing on during sex, a skirt that could be pushed up, a thong that could be yanked aside. I liked the idea of a barrier, of offering my body to someone but still retaining a part of myself in defiance of the act, so that no matter how far I went I never lost myself completely.

Sloan put a hand between my legs, running her fingernails over the flesh of my inner thighs. She moved her fingers over my clit and pushed one of them into me, curving it up toward my belly button, then another. She felt my sharp inhale and leaned down close, feeling my breath for a moment before putting her mouth against my ear.

"Does your boyfriend not do anything like this?"

I thought about sex with him, with all the boys I'd been with, the same every time. How I would cling to their sweat-bathed skin and feel lonely, take a vacation from my body, practice amateur telekinesis on the hands of the clock. Buck my hips against them and think about all the calories I was burning at the same time, about how my ass must look from behind. No matter how much light there was they always fucked you with their eyes closed. Blindly stabbing accomplishment. Boys didn't touch you to make you feel.

But this time was different. This time I stayed where I was.

I could feel my blood rising to meet her touch, taking off in small whirlpools beneath her fingers. I pressed my face into her neck and breathed her in. The spicy mélange of vodka and crushed cigarettes and men's cologne made me feel even more drunk. If this was sex, I'd never had sex before. This was a type of opened up it felt safe to be.

Sloan removed her fingers and worked them back in just as swiftly, this time with a third, then a fourth, knuckles pressed hard against my labia. She rolled on top of me, spreading my knees apart with her weight, and slowly started to push in the tip of her thumb. A hot rush of pain shot through me as I stretched to accommodate her large palm. A sudden *pop* and a sharp sting told me she had gotten wrist deep. She curled her fingers around her thumb to make a fist, knuckles up against some deep, thick-muscled part of me that seemed to push right against my lungs, making my breath short. A salty black tear escaped my eye.

"Does that hurt?"

I could feel my heartbeat resonating in her clenched fist, a heavy blood pound in the hard knot of center. She started to slowly open and close her hand inside me, pumping an imaginary stress ball.

"No."

I choked back the saliva that had gathered at the base of my throat as she started to pulse her hand faster, manipulating my body like a marionette.

She twisted her wrist and the last string holding me back snapped like a film cut and my body gave. My muscles seized up, sucking her deeper into the vacuum of my pelvis as she opened her hand to feel the waterfall of hot, viscous cum. A million pinpricks of white light exploded against my eyelids and the tide fell away just as quickly as it had risen.

She eased her hand out of me slowly, hollowing me out. The room had gone dark. Night wind blew in through the cracked window, mixing cold air with the attic's even warmth. I could still feel the ghost of her fist inside of me, the phantom weight of her body on mine. I was heavy and sunken, like sediment piled at the bottom of a lake. The dark wells of her irises were shot through with shimmering fiber optic veins.

"Let me get you some water," she said, kissing me on the cheek. She lifted herself off me and disappeared into the moonlit hallway.

"I'm on my period," said the girl whose name was Nik.

"Whatever."

I pushed her back on the rain-soaked lawn chair, pulled her pants and underwear down around her ankles and put my mouth directly on her clit. Normally I would have done some kind of foreplay or something, some running of the lips and teeth over her inner thighs, tracing the lines of her labia with the tip of my tongue, but I decided that would take too much time and anyway I didn't like her like that. She had just spent god knows how many minutes going down on me so logically this was what came next, and besides that I was stuck on a roof.

When it came to one night stands I always preferred going down on girls to just about anything else. Half was just the experience of it, my tongue inside a girl's cunt, the taste of it sharp and humid-sweet, but the other was the fact that it let me off the hook from doing anything else – looking them in the eye, saying the right thing at the right time, doing anything that could be meaningful at all. I'd plant my face between their legs and become my mouth, tidal blood and reverberating moans, and connected that way I would disappear. The intimacy paradox: as physically close as you can get to someone, drinking from their center, while being a million miles away. I know this because I always feel intensely, irrevocably alone on the receiving end, my head remote and solitary on the sweaty pillow, in a completely different orbit than the person whose face is stuck between my legs, working her ass off to make me come.

"I'm old enough to be your mom," Nik had said earlier at the bar.

These girls. It wasn't the first time someone pointed out that she could be my mother, all proud of it. As if age were all it took. It was always punctuated by some kind of sleazy smirk, half patronizing, half *I still got it.* Like they'd pulled off some type of advanced magic trick by being desired by someone younger. Why did they do that to people they wanted to sleep with? Obviously they thought it was cute in some taboo teacher-student sort of way, but I didn't see how they didn't see it was insulting. Who the hell hears "Oh, you're still a baby!" and immediately feels the need to drop her panties? But maybe that was the trick.

I didn't think I was going to be able to get Nik off. Her body rose and fell with my movements and her breath shuddered like it was supposed to but my jaw was starting to ache and I felt the familiar pull beneath my tongue, that dull throb that reminds you it's a muscle after you've already overworked it. But it must not have felt too bad – her fingers were intertwined with the loose coils of my hair, damp with rain and sweat, pushing me deeper into the dark wire of her pussy. I decided she was just drunk. I certainly was. After the caipirinhas we'd had at least eight more cocktails apiece, three at Cubbyhole, two at Phoenix and three more at B-Side before she worked up the courage to invite me back home. I felt a lull in her breathing and a moment later she pulled me up by the shoulders.

"Wanna get off the roof?"

"Okay."

We staggered through the trapdoor, somehow without decapitating ourselves, and down the stairs to her room. Nik lived in a grown-up apartment on 9th St. & Avenue D, a friend's place she was crashing between moves, apparently. She was small and muscular and tan, wild and untethered, with ripped jeans and an eyebrow ring a couple decades late but on her looked charming. All of these were things that made me decide to sleep with her that night. In the bar I had asked what her plans were for Pride weekend.

"It's this weekend?" Both eyebrows up in genuine surprise.

I felt warm toward her. I wondered if she even knew what city she was in that week. She'd just been telling me about a filmmaking seminar in Berlin, a music festival in Budapest, a weekend in Krakow where unfortunately she did not get to see the fire-breathing iron dragon. At that moment it was imperative that I figure out how to live like she did. Whether or not I even had the capacity was irrelevant.

Nik removed the rest of my clothes and threw them in a corner, grimy and soaked through from rolling around on the roof. She spread my legs, situated herself between them and slowly started to work her hand into me.

"You need lube," she said, getting up to her desk drawer.

"What kind do you have?" I was drunk, but I wasn't careless. I'd had enough of these New-Agey lesbians and their idea of lube, everything from aloe vera to olive oil to the shitty KY left over from when they used to fuck men.

"Oh my god, it's lube."

"But what kind? Let me see."

"Seriously?"

"Yes."

She exhaled and turned on the overhead light. My eyes split open long enough to catch the words "glycerin free" on the label floating in front of my face. At least I wouldn't be getting a yeast infection. Okay. I thought about asking for gloves next but stopped myself because I didn't want to come off more finicky than I already did, and also I was sure she didn't have them.

She turned the light back out, arched her small body over mine and resumed threading her fingers into me one by one. It was easier with the lube but still uncomfortable. I felt something jab at my bladder and clenched up tighter, and realized how badly I had to pee. Did I actually need to pee or was she just an excellent G-spotter? I was too drunk to know. But I was impaled on her arm. She doubled back and squirted some more lube onto her submerged hand with the free one. I felt the tiny sting of her thumbnail rind past my inner labia, then the breaking stretch of the wide part of her palm. It hurt and it didn't get better. My body refused to open, absorb the hand into its matter like rocks in a glass of water, but instead resisted it fiercely, pushing her out. She pushed back harder. I tried visuals: inflating balloons, dome-shaped ceilings, a tent going up, anything. Nothing worked. At that point all I wanted to do was go home but it seemed against protocol to say so, so I just told her I was sorry I couldn't and we both passed out gratefully.

In the morning I woke up with a headache on the right side of the bed, the wrong side. I looked over at Nik, sleeping. Her brown curls were fanned out over the pillows, tan limbs sticking out every which way from the tangle of sheets. I touched her hair, softened by a golden tint in the light. She was beautiful and far away from me. I peeled my wet clothes off the floor, silently congratulated myself on not peeing in her bed and made my exit.

Waves of heat rise off the asphalt into the plain, primary-color horizon. Kids named Brian or Sarah or Kaylee – a name like that, no more than two syllables – dressed in pink and khaki and powder blue sit cross-legged in the driveways and play with plastic things. The faint CH-CH-CH-CH *of sprinklers over each manicured lawn. Sturdy green plastic mailboxes stand guard, some with one slot for newspapers and some with two. I wonder about the two-slot mailbox people who couldn't come up with anything better to do with their money, because everyone knows the newspapers only come one at a time.*

The guy next door has one driveway and four different vehicles. Two reasonable cars, one motorcycle and one Corvette. He takes the Corvette out for a spin around the neighborhood every Sunday. Sometimes he polishes the motorcycle. Some days he mows the lawn twice. Today is one of those days. His mailbox is one of the ones with two slots.

I think about doing something. I think about going somewhere, for fifteen straight minutes. You used to go to the park, you told me, when you still lived here and couldn't sleep. You'd go under the bridge and watch the river, dirty and slow, car headlights splitting open the dark from above. Peaceful down there, you said. The good kind of silence.

I think about going there but if I went I don't think I would go home.

I go to the mall instead.

Bright stretchy leopard print shirts for $2.99 puncture the greyspace. Scattered kiosks with bored dark-skinned men offering cheap ear piercings and tongue rings topped with spiky neon koosh balls. Stick-legged girls with straightened hair and too-bronze foundation. Acne-scarred boys who smell like pot. Stained sweatpants. Creaking strollers. The Starbucks has a rollercoaster-sized line.

I get in it.

There was something I read once that said coffee raises the level of acidity in your stomach, so if you drink too much you can throw your natural pH balance out of whack. I consider whether the sour ache in my stomach is the beginning of a caffeine ulcer, or something else. This other thing I read about psychosomatic illness, how your mind can literally make you sick. I used to not believe this but I think this is how it's possible to die of heartbreak.

I order black coffee, make a note to investigate the ulcer.

The hangover settled in behind my eyeballs as I staggered down the stairs of the building into the sunlit street. God the street was bright. Even with my shades on it was impossibly bright. The taste of Nik had soured in my mouth. I looked in my bag for some gum, a mint, anything to chew, but only came up with a lonely Newport drifting half-crushed at the bottom. I fished it out and lit it, inhaling deeply. I felt a little better. Smoking menthols always seemed to eradicate the need for breath mints.

Two girls stood close together under an awning, their faces half hidden by shadow. One of them was wearing a pastel dress and vanilla perfume and the other was dressed in jeans and red flannel. The flannel girl leaned in for a kiss and the vanilla girl threw her arms around her neck, and when she did that her fake Chanel bag fell into a puddle on the ground. I must have stopped for a long time to watch them because when I snapped back a man was asking me for money. I told him I didn't have cash, which was true, except everyone says that and he's used to people lying. He yelled obscenities at me all the way down the street. I hoped he would notice the bag in the puddle, but when I turned back around both he and the girls were gone.

As I neared my building I saw him walking up the sidewalk, the same man I saw every morning I got up early and ran out for coffee: all 95 pounds of him, making his way up the street at a glacial pace and always with a different kind of heavy thing on his shoulders, four weeks' worth of laundry or empty paint cans or dirty bottles in a punctured trash bag. This time it was the laundry again, full to bursting. He was approaching me slowly where I'd dropped down to relight my cigarette, in the little nook between the dentist's office and the bodega where for some reason the bums never sat. His eyes, deeply entrenched in their sockets, shone out from his face, a sad, sallow brown with the skin stretched so tight you could see the latticework of his bones. He continued to place one foot in front of the other with the most deliberate caution, as if approaching a poisonous snake whose venom he wanted to extract.

I was rooted to the spot, hypnotized by the motion. It almost felt like something bad would happen if I turned my back or walked away, severed the invisible thread that was pulling him closer. Like one thoughtless movement could snap something cosmic.

Finally, after what seemed like hours, he stood grounded in front of me. He peered straight down into my eyes.

"Are you okay?" His words came out slow and metered as his walk.

"Yeah…why?"

"Usually people who smoke are not okay."

These street prophets. I felt the urge to scream. Or cry. Or seize him by the shoulders and explain, sit him down next to me in the nook and pour out all the absurdities in my life that had merged together to point me in the direction of smoking right here. I wanted to do that, and thank him, and stub out the cigarette and apologize, but instead I just sat there, staring at the small, earnest face pinched by worry and time, unable to collect any words.

And then I felt angry. I thought I looked calm, sitting there. Serene even, my legs at easy angles, eyes anonymous behind the cokehead shades. What kind of tragic pain was I exuding, to make complete strangers with excruciating bags of laundry atop their shoulders stop to ask if I was okay? I remembered the thing I read about the interconnectedness of the universe and felt a wave of paranoia. Maybe the laundry angel really did know my thoughts. Maybe he was a prophet of some kind. A real seer, one of those rare humans blessed with extrasensitivity, the ability to detect universal soft shifts, to feel the movements of other worlds pressed in on the sides of ours. Whose soul stirred from other souls stirring. His eyes, unblinking and dilated and liquid dark, held my gaze.

I stared back at him with as much presence of self as I could manage in my infinite headache and said nothing, breaking inside. I felt like a sinner in the temple, a failure at keeping even the simplest of secrets, the pillow over my stomach slipping out from under my shirt, stolen pearls scattering across the shop floor. Who did I think I was, anyway? What was I approximating? He gave me another peace-filled look as if to say, *It's okay. You still have time.* I got a hold of myself when I felt the forgotten cigarette prickle at my fingertips.

Without another word he turned and began walking up the street just as slowly as he'd approached, as if the act of walking were more for ritual than actually getting somewhere. I wondered where he made his money. Where he lived. Whether he took care of anyone, his siblings or his mother, if anyone in his house was sick and if he moved a bit faster when getting them things. At a certain moment he paused and turned, looking back at me, and took a tentative step in my direction as if he'd forgotten to say something else, but before anything could happen I stood up, brushed the street dust off my ass and took off toward the door.

Later, freezing water dripping over my chicken-skinned body in the shower, I realized the laundry angel had walked away in the same direction he'd come from.

I usually get good ideas when I smoke cigarettes. Sometimes I stand on my balcony and stare at the clump of ivy creeping up the neighbor's wall and smoke because I have nothing to do. Then I'll get an idea and it'll come in a FLASH *of inspiration, like that* IN ALL CAPS, *but I usually forget it before I can write it down. When that happens I have another cigarette in the same spot and try to coax it to come back.*

Sometimes I worry if I quit smoking I'll quit having good ideas.

My downstairs neighbor is a supermodel and I remember this when I reach for the pita chips. I wonder if she watches me from her deck when I do yoga badly in the living room. I've never been to her place but I'm pretty sure she can see mine through the window. I don't know if she does yoga herself but I do know she drinks PBR *tallboys alone on humid nights and for some reason I find that endearing.*

My other neighbor has constructed a miniature forest getaway in her backyard, this huge lush canopy of green walled in by bricks and concrete. The rain is falling into it and I can almost see the plants swelling with water, absorbing the droplets through their cells.

The tinny sound of rain on the fire escape reminds me where I am.

A woman in black lingerie stares out her window in the next apartment complex and I think she might be looking at me but I'm not sure. I blow a cloud of smoke in her direction and stare back at her until her image distorts, then go to bed. In the morning I go outside with my coffee and see her standing in the same place but as it turns out she is a cleverly constructed floor lamp.

Some nights I go to the bar down the street with a book and annex a table, it's too dark to read but I order a drink and strain my eyes anyway. Someone always wants to know what I'm doing there all alone and I tell them I got stood up on a date because I don't feel like explaining. They call my fictional date an asshole and say he doesn't deserve me over and over until I start to feel bad for the guy even though he doesn't exist.

The best thing about cash only bars is that you don't have to wait around to close a tab long after you're ready to leave.

On the way home I think about this episode of The Office in which Jim attaches a red wire to Dwight's computer and Dwight follows it all through the office and outside up a telephone pole, and I remember it being really funny but also really sad, like that's what all this is basically, a red wire. You pull at it and follow it along uprooting things until finally you end up on top of a telephone pole, or somewhere else really pointless.

The walk to work is thirty minutes every time, piano music in my ears. Always instrumental to make me forget where I'm going. All the way up 11th, detour to 10th where 11th brakes for a church at 4th Avenue, up 10th, cross Broadway, my hoodie always gets caught on the same rogue wire sticking out from the chainlink fence. I wake up in front of the bright lights and red neon and every time it's what am I doing here, every time like the first.

You can't work in a sex shop forever.

But this place wasn't Eden. Instead of malt liquor under the counter, three a.m. closing shifts and uppers to help, there were sales incentives, policies about time theft and a whole plethora of official fine print that made the whole thing look like something approaching a career instead of a purgatorial gig for the desperate. I didn't get into med school like the plan was. I didn't come up with a work of genius like the hope was. I didn't even disappoint my mother like I should have, her phone calls no longer containing the telltale sighs that felt like a degree marker for her belief in me. I didn't end up doing anything except this one thing I was qualified to do. I had four years of credit there too. I was living the cautionary tale of the classically trained musician who wound up an insurance salesman. Like they all do, says the drunk dad at the dinner table. But it's a less pathetic thing here, in a city that tries to eat you alive, because we all end up doing the same. Everyone understands when your answer to the intrusive Now What? devolves from the younger, grander Everything into the simple *survive.*

And here we all were, selling elegantly packaged sex toys to entitled strangers. Cosmo-soaked *Sex and the City* girls in bonebreak stilettos giggling over the Rabbit, lining up for the pink Elastomer one from the show even though it's a worse quality material than the newer silicone ones, doesn't matter how you try to explain. Crashing drunk straight couples with money clips and bleached teeth who'd had one too many gin martinis, forgot themselves at the door and now thought it hilarious to turn on everything in the store, everything but each other. Hairy-knuckled hands palming Pilates-firm asses. The young couples who would later become them, tasteful J.Crew-clad women with equally tasteful highlighted hair – neutral, classy, not too much – heaven forbid she ever be too much – nude-manicured nails, black pumps – can't afford Louboutins yet but she'll get there – their gelled and cologned investment boyfriends acquired through a friend or Match.com who haven't quite grown out of their college days, who want to keep their nice pressed work shirts and beer pong tables in equal measure.

These couples are always looking for something to Spice Things Up, as they say, it's a heartbreaking thing to say it that way, so young and bored already. Maybe he needs to pay more attention to her clit, maybe that's it, maybe this one-speed vibrating thing will do the trick? How about this one babe, what about this? Thing after thing after thing, looking for the best deal for the least amount of money, you guys don't have any discounts, do you honey. Once I had to spend fifteen minutes convincing a group of college boys that lube for anal sex was a necessary thing. They were astonished to learn that assholes are not self-lubricating. Almost insulted they were being expected to spend money on pleasure, hers especially, when sex was the oldest pastime of the world. Look at his parents, he bet they didn't need some kind of fancy apparatus, he bet she was perfectly fine with whatever god endowed. They've been married forty years and they're still in love, they kiss each other all the time for christ's sake, his father buys her jewelry for all the important dates. She used to cut the crusts off his sandwiches when he was a kid, made all his Halloween costumes by hand. One year she even made him a Tin Man out of foil. There was no way Mom needed a vibrator. But was there? Oh fuck now he's thinking about it. Oh fuck stop stop stop. Now every single thing in here, Jesus fuck, did she want that? There's no innocuous place to deposit his gaze, the horse bits and the butt plugs have taken on a new disturbing context, he's changed her, now everything is her –

Who was she before Mother, who is she besides Mother, would he have wanted to know that woman, could he have turned her on if he weren't her son?

And this is the fantastic part, when their faces flush crimson and their eyes sparkle wild, because the more you think about not thinking about something the more you end up thinking about it, and you can always tell, in the sex shop, which of the flustered young men have accidentally started getting boners thinking about their moms.

Something else about airports: half the reason to go to them is for the shops. Airport shops are like tiny condensed surface peels of life suspended in a jelly, and they're amazing. Being inside one is an almost cinematic experience, a simple sugar dreamscape in technicolor time, the screaming magazines, hot pink lipstick you won't believe helps you lose weight fast how to tell if he's cheating the clock: ten best antiaging products, dinner by six ways to jazz up your home this winter wonderland. They're another dimension. Then there are the other ones, those fancy little outposts with real chocolate and perfume and neck pillows from cool-eyed countries, pashminas and heavy watches, things you never go out of your way to buy unless you're late buying a gift for someone temporarily forgotten, or too hungry to care about dropping eight dollars on a bag of cranberry-maple pistachios, or something else ridiculous.

But the perfume. An airport is essentially a perfume emporium, and next to top-shelf liquor or a carton of cigarettes – we appreciate our deaths wrapped in nice packages from the duty free, thanks – perfume is the go-to gift. European people, whenever they go anywhere, always bring perfume for the family. It's at the level of tradition but I've never found it anything short of bizarre. People spend years searching for their signature scent, and here come these harried businessmen buying Miss Dior Chérie for their colleagues' teenage daughters and Trésor for their aging wives. Trying to guess their constitution through suggestive packaging and a spritz into the ether. It's beautiful really. You've only met her once at a party but somehow you're certain she's more Hypnotic Poison than Light Blue. A total shot in the dark for such an intimate thing.

Sloan, I knew, liked spicy, traditionally masculine scents that didn't show off all at once but pinpricked themselves into your nasal cavity, tobacco, leather, crushed grass and vetiver, sharp and deep but also somehow clean. I walk over to the men's shelves. Where the majority of women's scents were built like works of rococo art, the glass diamond-cut and bejeweled and filigreed, looking all manner of countess the wearer is supposed to feel, the men's were selling stoicism. Square geometries, blocky texts, dark glass. Rows of them. They looked more uniform than the women's.

What did Sloan use to wear? I examine the shelves, trying to think of it. The bottle that had lived in our bathroom was cut wider at the bottom and a dark green-blue. Three of those here, and that was matching the exact description. Maybe it was blue-green. I try for more details and it comes up different then, cerulean, the whole thing a cylindrical sort of a shape. I think back to the bathroom, the water-splashed mirror, half-empty jars of creams and spilled powders, the vapor-warped Rothko peeling off the wall. Our respective bottles had stood side by side on the sink. Mine was a dark smoky glass, purple. What was next to it? I look at the shelves once more.

Nothing.

How stupid. Not only was I going to throw a wrench in her life, I was about to do it with a stock gift in hand. What a fucking insult. Besides that, fragrance was lost on Sloan. Whatever she'd worn, Dior or deodorant, had just blended with her body base to smell more like her anyway, of stale smoke and the toxic sweats, the metallic blood scent of rust and rain.

I leave the perfume alone and head straight for the bookshelves in Hudson News. The books were organized more or less the same way. There were the customary chick lit confections, bright pink and white covers with lipsticks and stilettos and martinis, the bubbly scripts spelling out this or that about Mr. Right or going wrong. I pick up a few of these and turn them over to look at the author photos. The women all looked like they did juice fasts and faked their orgasms. Next to them were the big dark thrillers with looming titles, featuring characters with plot-convenient gifts or faults who for some reason had six hours to save the world from impending demise. The men responsible for these wore thin scarves or conductor hats and looked solemnly off into the distance. Then a row of literary bestsellers at 30% off, a threadbare Best Of section according to TIME.

Why no one does a Worst Of section is a mystery to me. Now that would be something to look at. A carefully curated collection of books that have not been critically acclaimed by anyone and never will be, that will never make it onto a required reading list, that have been stamped with no awards, have not been hailed as worth the time by any tastemaker committees, backed by no celebrity endorsements, maybe even lacking a description to begin with. Featuring absolutely zero plot, unbelievable narrators and issues relevant to no one. Worst Of Contemporary Fiction. Imagine the possibilities. Worst Of Art & Design. Light installations designed to short circuit, a touring exhibit of frames without pictures and a line of high-end umbrellas made of paper maché. Worst Of Nonfiction & Memoir. Featuring kindhearted satanists and drug addicts who are not sorry. The Complete Worst Of Poetry. Sixteen forms of line breaks to drag out the failings of the miserable human heart.

On the far left of the top shelf I spot Patti Smith's *Just Kids*. Immediately I feel relieved. I spent my entire life not knowing who Patti Smith was. I mean I did, in a cursory way, but even though I had inherited them I never sat down with her records, never let them take me anywhere. She was real, though, I knew that much. You could just see it in her. The cover was shiny black, with a black and white photo of her and Robert Mapplethorpe. Robert had his eyes sort of closed, his head slightly tilted up as if to receive the divine light. Patti's bangs were over her forehead and shading her left eye, the right one looking straight into mine. There was something very christlike about them, something that made me feel like I could trust their eyesight. But she was the one looking at me.

I stand up on tiptoe to reach her, the last copy, fold her under my arm and head to the register.

Every month I make a calendar on butcher paper and nail it to the wall. Every day I look at the calendar for longer than normal in case I'm forgetting an important date, a deadline or someone's birthday. I worry that things will roll off me because I'm not all the way conscious.

Perhaps itself a form of consciousness, that I have that paranoia.

Every day I write down one thing I did in the little square. If I write I write down the number of words that I wrote. Sometimes it's seven hundred and sometimes it's seven. The seven are usually harder to come up with. If I read I write down the number of pages I read. If I step on the scale I write that down too. I write down 123 and 121 and 127 and wonder which are the parts of me that keep expanding and contracting to make all those numbers possible in one day.

I write down the crazy things too.

For example:

Last week I almost bought a goddamn candle, for $7. They have all these candles for different things, any area of your life that needs help. Motivation Creativity Sex. There's even one that says Manifest A Miracle. Is that the emergency button for candles? I'm tempted by it but think it should probably be reserved for the terminally ill, young kids with cancer and people going bankrupt.

Anyway.

Every time I go to Whole Foods I stalk the Money candle. It's green and smells good. Like citrus and clove. Like things that are supposed to get you excited about making money. I place it in my basket every time, then take it out. I do this once or twice, wanting to ask the universe for a raise, or another job, but then there's the reality of spending $7 on a fucking candle.

I walk away, itself a form of asking.

After Krista left, Mischa insisted we get back out into the dating world and plug up our bleeding hearts with other human beings. She didn't say it like that, and either way it was a terrible idea, but at that point I was into anything that would help distract her. She was inconsolable. She thought Krista had been The One despite heaping evidence to the contrary. I personally believed that anyone who stood a chance at being The One wouldn't have had their bags packed before they said their final words, or threatened to take the so-called love of their life to small claims court over something as silly as a month's rent, and I told her so. That wasn't The One, that was just someone, and either way not anyone worth it. But she was having none of it. There was Mischa with her enormous effusive heart, always striving to see the best in people and give them the benefit of the doubt. She simply refused to believe that her ex was a huge asshole, and I couldn't help but love her more for it.

"What is the point of even attempting another relationship right now? It's not like they don't all end the same way. You'd just be starting a new way to get there."

She stared at me.

"You need to think about how fucked up that is, what you just said."

Was it? I understood that being self-protective was an unpopular idea, but at this point a split seemed more like an inevitability than a risk. Inga cheated on my brother after five years of marriage and hadn't even attempted to lie. As much as lying is a sorry shot at saving your own ass, at least it shows you care enough about the consequences to manipulate the reality of what you did. Krista checked out after only three years, placing the amethyst ring quietly on the kitchen table and offering no explanations. Both lasted longer than the year and change Sloan and I spent together so I couldn't imagine what that must have been like, the weight of time sitting heavy on the weight of blood, squeezing it through microscopic cracks in the bones. In the wrong hands, love was fucking dangerous.

But I couldn't talk about how I felt because no one had room for pessimism when it came to this sort of thing. It was all supposed to be *Believe* and *Be Open* and *You'll Find Love When You're Ready*, as if when you put all the parts in their right places love was the thing that you won, a carnival prize from the mad psychiatrist. The ready thing seemed crazy. Who thinks about preparing themselves like a dinner table, ticking off points on some mental health checklist before their heart can be considered acceptable for public display? Believing, wanting, being, all those are offerings, not forms of currency that ensure a guarantee. And who the hell is ever ready. You fix one thing and then another thing breaks, this is how the world's survived. Imagine humanity plodding on this whole time with nothing to fix. And open, how far? Tiny fissure for a glimpse inside or full split to hold half in each hand? I couldn't imagine meeting a girl in a bar and telling her *I need someone to die with*, though occasionally I did it, interpreting her hands on me as a reassurance, her breath a living poem. I wondered if there was some kind of support group for the healthy coping mechanism-averse, or like an Emotional Cutters Anonymous Mischa and I could go to. *Hi, we're here with a bleeding heart problem. We need to carry a bucket around wherever we go or else we'll get kicked out of every place with white tablecloths.*

Regardless, we decided to try OKCupid. The experiment was, I would write her profile and she would write mine, and then we'd compare. The thing about online dating is you can't put too much thought into it because the whole thing is designed for failure. How are you supposed to accurately represent yourself in an online profile? It's hard enough to do in real life, where you have to keep making sure it's Real You speaking and not Nerve-Wracked Self-Sabotaging You, let alone on a self-made advertisement where you're free to paint as wild a picture as you please in an attempt to convince someone you're not a total lunatic and they should consider falling in love with you. Everything I thought of writing sounded ridiculous. *Six things you can't live without.* Depends on the mood I'm in. Are we being literal? Should I be one of those faux-clever douchebags who write Air, Water, Food here? Is it too superficial to list Lipstick, Zit Cream, Black Eyeliner? What if I were honest and wrote Vodka, Sleeping Pills, An Ever-Present Shred Of Self-Doubt? The thing was a death trap no matter what you did.

After she realized I'd written "fun-sized power lesbian with Jew fro seeks same," Mischa changed her password and crafted something so clever and quirky and appropriately unpretentious it ended up landing her a bunch of dates, with everyone from a comedy writer to a nude art model to a dental hygienist. We would rehash the dates the following day over beers, zooming in on every little detail that would help determine whether the girl would end up in the Yes No or Maybe pile. Mischa would then speculate on what would happen next, saying she "felt something" for this person and "I don't know, I can really see myself with her."

"But *how*? She thought Rick Moody was the frontman of a death metal band."

"So? She's really cool. And she's sweet. And she's not the only person who doesn't know who Rick Moody is."

How she did that, came up with the ability to feel things for all these girls, I couldn't begin to know. It wasn't that she necessarily felt something like the real thing, because that seemed impossible, but she was willing to give everyone a chance. I wished I could do that, if for nothing more than the fact that she was having more sex than I was. Instead I would find a million reasons not to see someone, everything from the fact that they were too short or did accounting or didn't read or ate meat or liked ice hockey. Small things. It wasn't hard for me to find something to take issue with, because deep down I knew I didn't want it to work. I didn't want to paste someone else over the hole Sloan had left inside me. I wanted it filled but with the right substance and I wasn't all the way prepared to understand that maybe I'd have to go through life that way, full of holes, holes upon holes and people making new holes that were just as unfillable, each successive Right Person carving out their piece ad infinitum, a human wiffle ball of rotten love.

The Right Person, I decided, would be butch. Butch enough that her hair would be short and she'd have muscles and no problem killing roaches and possibly a neck tattoo, but not so butch that the archaic gender binary dictated everything in her line of vision. This butch girl would have already run through scores of femme girls but none would have been to her liking because she found them too predictable. She would want a real partner, the right complement to her life and personality, someone who spoke her language and knew when to not speak. A girl who didn't hide her wounds under sleeves and makeup but wore them like jewelry, her hair rough and lipstick dark, whose only decidedly feminine quality was her warmth, but only if you earned it.

Enter, me.

We would get each other's jokes and finish each other's sentences, not in the cheesy TV way but in a way that meant we each occupied a side of the same thought, opposite one another in the two-way mirror. Sipping glass after glass of whiskey, wine, whatever there was, keeping pace with each other, eyes safe across the table, her hand on my back as we walked out of the bar. We'd exhaust ourselves with the talking and only then would we realize we were worth each other's silence, each other's bodies, and then we would soften to each other, first kiss incandescent as liquid gold. I wanted to fall in love so badly it made me sick.

> *You should message me if:*
> You have strong shoulders.
> And something to carry.
> You speak my language.
> And know when to shut up.
> You can close your eyes.
> And then hold them open.
> You have so much inside of you it's splitting the seams.

I left that alone, what Mischa wrote, and gave it a shot. The whole thing wrapped up with two dates, one fumbling fuck and one disastrous wine tasting, where I got accidentally drunk and threw up on her shoes. I decided that was all I had room to deal with and deleted my profile soon after.

Then there was Atalanta.

Atalanta was nutmeg and long hair and a laugh so loud it shook tiny dust clouds off the ceiling. Atalanta always made you late to German. She'd pull up in her sputtering Citroën and make you climb through the window because the passenger door wouldn't open. Atalanta wore coarse woven ponchos and smoked Ecstasy herbal cigarettes because she thought they were healthier and her forehead was always too shiny, even though mom bought her powder for Christmas once. She was wiry and agile, spry. Hers was a body built for scaling.

Atalanta made you bracelets from Fimo beads and twine stolen from her mother's crafting table. Her mother was an old time hippy lady, unpinned and lovely, one of the ones time forgot. She had a shop with batik prints and herb tinctures and Buddhas. I found three bracelets in the drawer, big thick beads with flowers and Om signs and birds etched in smoky script through bottle glass greens and ultramarines. I took one, wearing it now. I don't think she would have minded.

Atalanta read to you sometimes on a big blanket in the yard as you passed a joint back and forth. I remember the pungent green smell as I played with chalk on the sidewalk, my hands in the dirt. She read you novels and what I imagine were books for school, proofread your assignments, your English not quite there, going slow so you could tease out the unfamiliar words. She would bring over whatever her mother concocted in the kitchen, things you'd never heard of let alone tasted, crumbly protein bars cobbled together from nuts and seeds, pastes made from legumes and spices with strong flavors, things that tasted like earth magic. She was with you, there.

These are the things you wrote about her, more or less, in the memorial book her mother had made, a wide, heavy hardcover where her family and friends could share their stories. There's a picture of her on the front, hair long and hanging dark, perched on one knee, grinning. That smile. Our mom once decided Atalanta was too long and christened her Ata. You know how Polish people like to make things small, make foreign names sound like ours. She was one of ours now. Becoming.

crushed grass and something sweet, girl-like, burnt sugar, hair soaked in incense and rain

my head on her chest under the night sky, the apples of her cheeks, golden

she wanted to trade names of constellations even though I didn't know the names of my own.

These are some of the things you did not write, the handwritten pages stuck in the center of the book.

Apparently you can read this book any which way, there's a key Cortázar outlined in the opening pages. You can go front to back like usual, if you have minimal patience for the unconventional, or back to front if you're the rare type of person who doesn't trip over empty space while trying to jog backward. Or you can go in the crazy order he suggested, chapter 73 to 1 to 2 to 116 and on and on that way, the idea being several books inside of one, multiple forms of the story spun out from the same arsenal of words.

I decide to try the normal way first.

Would I find La Maga?

God damn it. I couldn't start like this. Of course if you say that you won't find La Maga. And even if you do find La Maga you'll have found her temporarily, physically maybe, either way not in the real sense and not in the way that you want, because even if you find La Maga you can never *find* La Maga. Regardless of what else happens in the book this is what the first sentence is saying. You start with a question like that and you already have an idea of your odds.

The first time I tried to read *Hopscotch* this way was that week at my mom's and I got further than this but not by much, maybe to the end of the first page, but the heat and exhaustion closed in before I could wrestle with the words that were so small and close together, so small and on top of each other, words upon words blending into inky Rorschach shapes –

Why do they do that, why do they print them so tiny. Why don't they understand that texts have psychosomatic effects.

"Have you ever tried to kill yourself?"

Sloan shifted onto her left elbow, the cigarette in her teeth dusting the duvet in a smattering of ash. The stilled smoke in the room made it look blue and frostbitten, awash in watercolor runoff.

I stared up at the ceiling. My body wasn't quite at equilibrium since the last fuck. I squeezed my legs together to quash the tingle in my clit, which felt inappropriate for this type of conversation.

"Yeah," I said. "Twice. Have you?"

"Of course."

"How?"

She was fifteen. She had just started school in America, which sucked because she barely spoke any English and her high school was in this rich suburban area where everyone was mean to her because she kept to herself for the most part and looked like a boy. The girls on the soccer team gave her a lot of shit because they thought she was gay and also because she played better than them. That part she couldn't help – training in Russia was no everyone's-a-winner hand-holding picnic. The coaches made you run until you puked and if "trying" was the best you had to give you might as well go invest in a pair of knitting needles, you'd be getting more use out of them in the long run. As for being gay, Sloan started dating the quarterback to prove she wasn't. The no-English thing wasn't a big deal since he didn't talk much anyway. She inexpertly sucked the first cock of her life in a bathroom stall at the Homecoming dance. Right before Thanksgiving the head bitch on the team tripped Sloan on purpose and made her sprain her ankle. She came home that day feeling completely nothing. She went downstairs to the basement where her dad kept his gun, in a safe she saw him pull a secret pack of Sobranies from once after he was supposed to have quit. She reached in there and took the gun out, the weight of it scary and reassuring in her hand, and put it right up against her temple. This was it, stupidly, amidst the broken lawn chairs and stained baby clothes in the moldy suburban basement. As she was squaring with that she heard footsteps on top of the stairs. Her little sister had come home early from school and was calling her name – *Sasha, Sasha!* – her real name, then appeared in the doorway to see Sloan holding the gun.

"I was just putting this away," Sloan said, moving to polish the barrel with her shirt. She placed the gun back in the safe and turned the combination several times, locking it out of sight. Tanya stared at her suspiciously, but smiled as Sloan made her way up the stairs and into the kitchen to make her a snack.

"I felt like such an asshole afterwards. I was really going to do it. I wasn't even thinking about Tanya. I wasn't thinking about anything. I had forgotten Tanya even existed until she was looking down at me from the top of the stairs. Isn't that a horrible thing?"

"Yeah," I said. "Well, I don't know. I feel like it happens all the time."

I'd lied to Sloan. I've never seriously tried to kill myself. I have tried to kill myself not seriously, meaning I had the idea and a half-assed attempt but never wholeheartedly committed. But she was right about that. Even when I put real thought into doing it I never considered my brother. I wondered if that was a horrible thing too. It's not like I'd come as RIGHT THERE as putting a gun to my head, but now I felt terrible in retrospect, the fact that it never crossed my mind, even in the most abstract way, what he would have thought.

There are a couple reasons I've never tried to kill myself.

One is that I got distracted. The first time I thought about killing myself was in a Steak & Shake. I was in high school and having milkshakes with my boyfriend. I remember mine was some strange kind of peanut butter strawberry swirl (why milkshake places put flavors like that together, I can't even begin to know) and the sky was a raw blue, such an insistent fucking BLUE you could barely even process what you were looking at, and I remember feeling crushed by something. Crushed and flattened by this nameless thing that just kept pushing harder and harder and I felt flatter and flatter until finally I got it: *I could push the weight off right now.* The realization was momentous. In the vast expanse of immoveable things, this was a thing I could move with my hand. It was surprising. It was exciting. It became the plan.

Immediately everything became clear. I became extremely interested in what my boyfriend was saying. The weird peanut butter and strawberry shake started to taste really good, and the sky was the most beautiful, welcoming thing I'd ever seen. To this day I could identify that exact piercing shade of blue. When we finished our shakes he drove me home because I said I had homework to do. I went upstairs and started getting ready.

I organized all the stuff I had into piles marked with names. Pictures, journals, everything had a label, who of my friends would get what. I turned on the computer and deleted everything I had written, everything I had saved. I didn't want to leave any suggestions, any clues that could be put together into a story. I wiped the whole thing clean and when I was done I went downstairs and got a bottle of vodka from the dining room and an assortment of pills from the medicine drawer, Advil and Percocet and my grandma's valerian root, no medical reason for that one except I remember wanting to die with a little piece of her. She was on the couch watching *Days of Our Lives.* She didn't speak any English but she had a pretty good handle on the story so far, the melodrama was easy to follow. I said goodbye to her silently as I walked up the stairs and prayed her memory was bad enough that she would just forget me.

I sat down on the floor cross-legged with the pills and the vodka. The wind was blowing in through the open window, that saturated cloud-strewn blue peeking in between the curtains like a Magritte sky. I opened up the first bottle, Advil. They're an ugly color but they taste good, I'm sure there's a lesson to be learned there. I shook ten into my hand, shifting them around so the sugar coat wouldn't rub off on my palm, then some Percocet, one valerian. Who knew if those were the right proportions. But this was it. I would die under that sky. I closed my eyes and shoved the pills in my mouth, not two seconds before I realized the distant rumble under the floorboards was the garage door opening. My mom had come home early from work. I panicked and spit the pills back into my hand, then ran to the bathroom to flush them down the toilet before rushing to hide the rest of my death accessories.

I wrapped my arms tight around my mother in the kitchen, let her feed me a day-old salad that went bitter in my mouth. After dinner we were quiet as we moved around each other cleaning up the dishes, until the bowl I was carrying shattered when it violently occurred to me I'd just deleted all my midterm papers.

"What about you, how did you try?"

"What?"

"How did you try to do it?"

"Oh, you know." I turned on my side, face to the wall. "One time wrists, once ammonia."

Sloan laughed in a weak sort of way.

"You wanted to feel it, huh."

"Who the hell wants to feel it?"

"People who do wrists and ammonia."

I said nothing and she went silent at my silence. Her fingers found my left wrist and started to move up and down the main vein, palm to tendon to forearm and back again. We stayed that way for a while, chests rising and falling in opposite rhythms.

"But you don't have any scars…"

I freed my hand from hers and tucked it under my stomach, then turned around and kissed her on the nose.

"I know, right? They make creams these days like you wouldn't believe."

The one time I called Sloan *Sasha* she had a fit.

It was a sweaty summer night and we were rolling. Crystal Method were playing in a renovated cathedral and my roommate's friend, a guy you'd never expect to come through on anything, approached us and asked if we'd like some E.

"Normally it'd cost you guys," he said. "But what the hell. Happy holidays."

I felt charged. I had never done ecstasy before and I couldn't have thought of a better place to try.

"Shall we, Sashenka?" I arched an eyebrow in mock seduction.

She shook her head, irritated.

"Don't call me that," she said.

I draped my arm around her.

"But you're so pretty."

She shrugged it off.

"You don't get it. I'm not that girl anymore."

I got it. She had worked so hard to not be Sasha and here I was dumping it back on top of her. Everything she'd gone through to kill off the weak parts of herself, I was descending to the river's bottom and dredging them up, vein blue and waterlogged, back to the surface. She didn't want to be Sasha because it meant *Aleksandra,* her birth name, the name the parents she had nothing in common with stuck to her, and especially not *Sashenka,* sweet and cow-eyed and diminutive, the kind of name that looked at the floor when given a compliment and wore frilly white socks with its sandals. But above all she didn't want to be Sasha because Sasha was feminine and Sloan associated femininity with weakness and the last girl to call her that had been Kate Moss.

Kate Moss was a total fucking mystery. From what Sloan described she was this willowy gorgeous night creature with a semi-respectable day job, legal something or other, but at night she would wrap up her long skinny body in dark flowing fabrics and shut down the Moscow night clubs, high on every drug known to man. I knew Sloan exaggerated when she described her but I wasn't sure how much and also didn't want to acknowledge the possibility that she might not be exaggerating at all. Apparently all Kate Moss ate was strawberry yogurt. She fed Sloan shitty 3-star cognac because it was cheap and anyway Sloan didn't care what she drank. She was seventeen and in love with her. She had met Kate Moss crying on a curb outside a club, uptight pinstripe office skirt climbing her thighs. Her ex-boyfriend was there with some other girl. Sloan sat close to her and lit her cigarettes, wiped away the black streams running down her cheeks. She's always had a thing for desperate strangers.

"Her real name's Kate Moss?"

"Of course not," Sloan said. "We just called her Kate Moss because she looked like Kate Moss."

Not only was Kate Moss beautiful, she was indestructible. One time she drove 90 miles per hour on the wrong side of the road just to see what it felt like. Occasionally she would play lottery pills with all the drugs in the house, shake them up in a bottle and pop a random one in her mouth, see if she could guess what it was before it began to hit. Even though she was gone, she remained something to compete with, the memory alive in Sloan's mind a black mark on my consciousness.

"I don't miss her," Sloan said. "She wasn't stable. I couldn't go home to her."

I supposed she meant that to sound reassuring but it sent a ripple of horror through me. It made me wonder whether that was what she wanted at all, to go home to someone. Whether the stability was something she knew she needed but didn't really want, like iron supplements or getting your blood drawn. She was home with me all the time and we were both sick with it, asphyxiating ourselves with the constant connectedness of our mouths, vodka and menthols and Marlboro Reds on the ever present base notes of strawberry yogurt and the occasional black Sobranie.

"Whatever," I said. "Let's do these drugs."

My pill was acid green and had a dolphin imprinted on it. Sloan had a pink one with a tiny mud flap girl. We popped them in our mouths in the bathroom at the same time and chased them down with water. I was relieved to have an excuse to drink water for the rest of the night, if only for the fact that we were both underage and getting alcohol anywhere was such a fucking ordeal it didn't even feel worth it. The summer before we had gotten kicked out of an MSI concert simply because I was holding a beer. Not even drinking it, just holding it for a friend who went to the bathroom and didn't want to put it down on the disgusting floor. I was livid. *Look*, I told the security guy. *This isn't mine. This is fucking Bud Light.* The very thought that I would risk getting kicked out of someplace because of Bud Light was so ludicrous I couldn't believe he would even suggest it, and I tried to make him see that. But he was having none of it. In America, being underage and within six feet of anything with an alcohol content is cause for alarm. I told him that by that logic, I already had a contact buzz from the liquor-soaked mosh pit so what difference did it make.

"You don't get it," I said. "This is the kind of thing that makes kids want to drink *more*."

He told me if I put up any more of a fight we would both get arrested. We had already gotten a warning from the lady security guard for fucking in the bathroom and holding up the line. Sloan had unzipped my tight blue dress – such a bright chemical blue it made your eyes hurt – and gone to work on me, but the problem was I could only spread my legs so wide because the dress was attached to garters which were attached to fishnets which were stuck in my boots and by the time I figured out how to maneuver my outfit the other girls in line had started throwing wads of toilet paper over the stall door.

"Fuck off, we're having a moment!" Sloan shouted to the line, which only increased the amount of toilet paper thrown over the door from every direction.

"Whatever," I said, pulling her out of me by the wrist and zipping myself back up. "Let's go. I can't even focus."

And thus we exited the stall, which is how I got suckered into holding my friend's shitty beer in the first place.

Of course after we got kicked out Sloan suggested climbing back over the fence into the smoking area, but the thought of doing that, especially while not wearing underwear, was only slightly less mortifying than the thought of getting kicked out again by the same bouncer, or worse, making him help me down from the fence my vagina would inevitably get impaled on. And I was pretty sure I did not look anonymous that night. In a sea of mall goth black-on-black, the cobalt blue dress and same-colored hair would be difficult to miss. Especially impaled on a fence.

"Fine," Sloan said. "If you don't think it's worth a shot, we'll just *go home*."

"Come on, babe. It's not the last time we'll get to see MSI."

I tried to sound like I believed what I was saying but I couldn't help thinking Kate Moss would have done it. Kate Moss would have hopped that goddamn fence and slipped through the tight-packed crowd of smokers like mercury, reached under her dress and pulled a joint out of her snatch. Kate Moss would have let Sloan finish fucking her in the bathroom, caught the wads of toilet paper flying over the door and thrown them back at the pissed off girls wet with her own spit and cum. Kate Moss wouldn't have been content to just *go home.* Kate Moss, whatever she would have done, wouldn't have been scared.

I used to think the cigarette burns on my arm were kind of cool. I remember what smoker-crammed patio I was on when I got each one, and when people with concerned expressions asked me what I'd been doing to myself I would just tell them Oh no, this is my smoking arm. Then show them my left arm, sans burns.

See?

Sometimes I walk around Washington Square Park and try to imagine it in black and white, all because of this one photo of Allen Ginsberg and Gregory Corso that showed up in my newsfeed between kale salad and engagements and for a split second I thought they were still alive.

There's something about black and white that always makes things look alive. Desaturating images distills them down to their bare souls. You take the skin off first, pull out the color and minutiae, everything the distractible eye has a tendency to focus on, and close in on the soul particle, the metaphysical skeleton, the smile that can snap elevator cables, the light behind the eyes, or the dark. There's no such thing as a flaw in a black and white picture. Every shadow, wrinkle, hair out of place is a pure, compounded thought. When we see the thing in person, crumpled in a subway puddle or spilling out of a tight dress in bulbous folds in the daylight, the first thing we want to do is look away. When it's in black and white, the only thing we want to do is look.

I think about whether seeing Washington Square Park in black and white is worth the trouble of a self-induced blackout and decide that it isn't.

I know how to do this but I won't write it here because I know someone will try.

Jack Kerouac was missing from the picture I saw. Jack Kerouac, the quintessential receiver, whose soul stirred from other souls stirring. Too drunk to play himself in Pull My Daisy and made to narrate it instead.

If Kerouac were alive today and had stayed in school. If Kerouac had put himself through a writing program. Kerouac with his crazy scrolls of text, drunk on whiskey and visions, rolling on about holy nowhere and giving everyone a headache. A collective of class-taught writers cutting the scribbled parts of Desolation Angels and telling him to tighten up his prose.

If Kerouac were alive today he would've given up on writing and started an emu farm.

It's getting harder and harder to talk about real things.

Some guy on the bench next to me is looking at me for longer than normal and I wonder what his problem is. I notice my sleeves are rolled up. I stand up and roll them down.

The only time I see in black and white is when I'm about to pass out.

I know it's going to happen when my stomach compresses into an airtight knot and pushes up into my esophagus, then my vision blackens at the edges and goes grainy, narrowing into a shrinking static tunnel before the film cuts and I hit the floor. Eventually I wake up to someone panicking and slapping me in the face, cold and sweaty with a head full of ants.

The first time I understood this was a thing that happened was on a trip to Poland, when I was nine. My mom had sent me there for the summer because she worried I was forgetting the language, which was true. I was already one of the weird foreign kids in my Midwestern elementary and had put forth every effort into becoming as American as possible, everything from scouring the thrift stores for mall designer castoffs to purposely getting C's on spelling tests. When I started actually making up Polish words and declining them as if they were real, she'd had it. I was shipped off to my aunt's in Krakow for the entire summer, where I blacked out for the first time in front of the fire-breathing iron dragon. One minute I'm drinking fizzy lemonade with the dragon, and next thing I know I'm spread out on a stretcher in the pitch dark, crammed into a set of too-small boys' pajamas with a crooked IV sticking out of my wrist. Drugged and chilled under the skin, with a heavy soreness in my back teeth like the kind that comes from sucking on an ice cube too long. No one was able to figure out what was wrong. Heatstroke or anemia, it was decided, and I was sent home.

At thirteen I blacked out in the middle of Easter Vigil, which, if you're Catholic, you know is the two-hour Mass before Easter Sunday you only suffer through if your parents make you or there are snacks afterwards. Jesus was getting crucified and I, in the throes of my middle school goth phase, had worn a heavy black velvet dress for the occasion. They were driving the nails into his palms and feet when I heard the siren hum in the back of my skull. The altar candles flared up and I felt the cavernous church stagger as I forced myself out of the pew, the tunnel connecting my temples squeezing shut. My mother dragged me out into the hall, laid me down on my back on the cold tiles and in a swoop of medical efficiency lifted my legs into the air at a 90-degree angle to force the blood back in my head, simultaneously exposing my ass, bisected by a cherry red G-string, to several worried members of the congregation. She said nothing about the event afterward, except to tell me that I was no longer allowed to be a vegetarian.

After several more times like this then years without incident I thought I'd grown out of it, but it happened again my first fall in Chelsea, where I never go. It was a lovely October night and I'd dragged Mischa to a reading at what used to be Bungalow 8. Even though you didn't need a key to get in anymore, No. 8 still retained its fair share of cheesy pretense, what with the fake palm trees and ceremonious checking of the guest list. The reading was in the record room upstairs, glossy wood everything and shelves of vinyl blanketing the walls, if your grandfather had a bachelor pad sort of feel.

"Addiction Literature" was the theme and Tony O'Neill was reading from one of his books, I think it was *Dirty Hits*. He was talking about shooting dope, poking the needle around in his sick and collapsing veins in shitty rest stop bathrooms, about how he was so close to going into his neck but something stopped him. There was something too grotesque about it, something just this side of psychically unbearable about pinning down the jugular, the life vein, and making it sit still long enough to swallow a needleful of poison. If he had been any kind of resourceful, I remember thinking, he would have tied up with the necktie he was wearing (had he been?) and driven right into it, the way Burroughs described, the way the old-time junkies who weren't afraid of anything did. A terrible thing to think at an addiction literature reading.

At any rate, something was happening. I was beginning to feel warm. The vodka soda in my hand was starting to taste metallic, like rubbing alcohol, and the heat of the room was closing in. Everyone who was anyone in so-called literary society was packed into No. 8 like sardines in a fucking can. There was an airbrushed blonde lady to my left holding a glass of white wine. I stared at her, using her as a focal point to calm my quickening pulse. Who were all these people, and what the hell did they know about addiction? Why was I the only one who looked ready to dissolve? And why was this woman drinking white wine, wine was $18 a glass, didn't she know the Stoli cocktails were free? Who the fuck paid for alcohol when there was alcohol for free?

Thoroughly mystified and increasingly ill, I looked around for a place to deposit my body. What I really wanted to do was lie down, spread myself out in all directions like a warm pâté, but there were people sitting and standing all over and I didn't think it would look good to collapse on the floor either, fucking social conventions. Back home you could collapse where you wanted, but this seemed like the type of place where an ambulance would be called.

Through my darkening vision I managed to spot an empty space on the couch next to Ted, Ted who I'd spoken to earlier when we were both craning our necks for people to entrap in conversation, Ted who was coming out with a legal thriller that winter and didn't mind that I'd never heard of him. He looked bewildered but said nothing. The guy next to him knit his eyebrows and started to chatter, probably something like *Oh, somebody's actually sitting there*, but I didn't hear him. I didn't care. My eardrums were already caught in the wind tunnel. My finger pads felt tipped with needles and I was no longer able to see color, the floor below me taking off in a sickening static roil.

Shit, I thought. I'm going to puke. Or die. I dry heaved. I felt the globules of sweat roll down my back, the slimy coldness of them, the fact that I probably looked like a junkie, one fresh out of rehab who couldn't stand to listen to the mechanics of doing drugs. At the very least someone who could've used a trigger warning. The event photographer was slithering around snapping photos and I thought about how absurdly horrible, but also how funny it would be to be photographed puking or dying, no filter. Maybe even glamorous in my thrifted Balmain coat. I locked my head between my knees and squeezed my temples together, counting each breath as my vision contracted in a steadily tightening pinhole to total dark. Fortunately Mischa found me, dead pale and on the verge of collapse, before I fell forward into a stack of hors d'oeuvres. She carried me out before we got the chance to hear Elizabeth Wurtzel.

"What would you do without me," Mischa said on the corner, flinging one of my dead arms over her shoulder and the other one into the street to attract a cab. I leaned into her neck, closing my eyes against the flickering lights. My forehead crashed against her collarbone.

"I don't know," I said. "Without, I guess."

"Yeah right."

A cab pulled up and she lifted me into it, tucking my coat in behind me as I plastered my cheek to the vinyl. She squished herself in beside the mass of fake fur.

"Don't tempt disaster," she said. "Not with your luck."

And then, "Crown Heights."

Something else about airports: people always wreak havoc on themselves. I mean they eat all manner of horrible food designed to give you heartstop they wouldn't normally eat, or at least wouldn't eat sober in broad daylight with other people watching. But in an airport, no one cares. You lock eyes with someone in the midst of their double bacon cheeseburger and extra large fries and there's this implicit understanding, sometimes even a knowing nod. *It's okay. Me too.* Which I'm pretty sure is a survival thing. You have to eat whatever's around with the highest calorie content because you never know when you're going to be able to eat again. When it's equally possible that you will be served a packet of peanuts for dinner or go crashing into the ocean, it just doesn't make sense to eat a salad.

The woman beside me is crunching her way through a box of chicken nuggets. Crunching, that is the word. These chicken nuggets are crunchy as hell. They have been deep-fried with a vengeance. Personally I am of the opinion that chicken nugget skin should not be crunchy, at least not that crunchy, but these resonate with such a deliberate, infernal crack it makes me wonder if even she is thinking about it, if at this moment she is taking it as a warning that her food is making such an unnatural sound. I picture the lipid molecules, microscopic grease balls floating around in her viscera, and think about the word, *lipid,* how the object recalls the sound, banana-shaped fat deposits emergency yellow on either side of a dissected frog.

Sloan didn't believe in fat content, or being health conscious, or counting calories. She adhered to the nebulous unscientific idea that there were Fat People and there were Thin People and if you were a Thin Person you could eat whatever you wanted and your body would magically maintain equilibrium on its own. A child of winter, she was under the impression that restricting food for any reason was insane. Supremely conscious of the fact that at that exact moment someone in Siberia had only a frostbitten carrot to contend with, everything she came up with in the kitchen was rich and artery filling, heavy with history and guilt. On the rare occasion she deigned to make a salad the romaine leaves were a barely visible seafoam green in the wooden bowl, the accompanying vegetables indistinguishable beneath a thick coat of mayonnaise.

"Who the fuck puts mayo on a salad?"

"Russians," Sloan said matter-of-factly, dropping a heaping mound onto my plate before loading up the rest with roast chicken and potatoes. I watched the mountain of lettuce begin its drooping descent under the avalanche of gloop and raised my fork. It was her fault I couldn't fit into any pants.

She pointed her fork at the mountain.

"What's wrong, you don't like my dinner?"

"Of course I do," I said. "But maybe we should be eating healthier."

Sloan and I had each put on at least thirty pounds since moving in together, not that I was suicidal enough to try weighing myself. At first I thought my pants had shrunk in the laundry when I had trouble squeezing into a size four, but at a certain point I could no longer blame the dryer for becoming a size twelve.

"But this is healthy," she said. "Look. Protein, veggies, and carbs. The pyramid thing. What else do you want?"

"Veggies don't count if they're floating in an ocean of trans fats."

Sloan's eyes went all the way black.

"Why don't you tell me what this is really about? You want to lose weight, is that it? Who do you want to lose weight for?"

History and guilt.

"Forget it," I said, stabbing my fork into the salad pile's white heart. "We can get diabetes together if that's what makes you happy."

It meant I would have to go on a secret diet, which annoyed me, but I was used to it. I'd done it for years when I still lived with my mom, throwing out lunches at school, throwing up whatever I ate into the toilet. The first diet I went on was in third grade. We had a unit about nutrition and twiggy Ms. Johnson mentioned that if you ate too much fat and sugar and cholesterol they would congeal into an insidious yellow cocoon around your heart and squeeze the life out of it little by little until you died. Naturally I was horrified. I was chubby already and the popular girls made fun of me enough as it was, making sure to remind me every so often that my stomach had more rolls than a bakery on Sunday. I avoided it in the mirror, it stung to look, but I felt them, one, two, three pillowy protrusions bulging over my pants in ascending order of size. One would hope that a bakery on Sunday had more than three rolls in the inventory, but that wasn't the way I thought then. One meal a day, I promised myself, until it was all gone. I needed to eat more like my mother did, black tea first and never more than half a cup of anything. Discipline. Moderation. Control. Those were the English words I needed to learn.

Determined not to die of being fat, I decided the fastest way to results was to stop eating. I didn't eat for an entire day at school and ended up with a cookie made of Crisco and chocolate chips shoved in my hands by the nurse, because my vision had tunneled in music class and I fainted on top of a piano. I went to bed that night imagining my little heart struggling under its fat coat, thinking about how ingesting just about anything was an affront to your whole body, how we let too much inside and we all die that way, of consumption. Repeat that behavior for the next fifteen years.

The woman pulls a packet of mayo out of the paper bag. She tries tearing it open with both hands but they're too greasy to grasp it properly so she pinches one corner and rips it open with her teeth (success!) and globs the mayo all over the remaining nuggets. Unfortunately it does not mute the crunch. I turn my music up louder – "Skinny Little Bitch," appropriately – but the crunch is now something my brain's repeating, keeping time on the inside of my skull.

The latte is enormous, ridiculous, unnecessary American coffeehouse size. Triple espresso, soy milk and a squeeze of almond syrup, that's what I was into drinking. Black coffee for you, anything else was a waste of time. You used to come here all the time in high school, did I? No, I said, looking around. It was different, you said. You could smoke inside and there was live music. It seemed like someone had turned the music off a long time ago.

You laughed.

Did you draw those on with a protractor?

The camera flashed when I put a hand up to cover my eyebrows.

The picture is blurry because my hands were moving but you can see the wire chairs, the patio, the thick knit of my gray sweater, white hands with black nail tipped fingers covering white face, long russet hair, black lowlights and dirty blonde roots, the color of dying leaves, botched drug store project.

I took out my cigarettes when you did and lit one, my first time in front of you, pulled the smoke in deep down my windpipe, worked it through my lungs and released it, slow and controlled, into the atmosphere. The way real smokers did.

Don't smoke, you said, exhaling.

I won't.

The wind picked up, scattering dirty napkins and ash across the patio.

For some reason the skin under my eyes had begun to break apart. It was delicate skin, translucent and thin like chiffon, that itched and burned when I rubbed my eyes and erupted in angry red rash when I attempted cream. When I smiled it bunched up under my lower lashes with the crackly toughness of aerated dough and aged me ten years. Sometimes I would stand in front of the mirror and smile and stop for minutes at a time, on and off, smile, relax. Like watching time accelerate and reverse.

Fuck it's cold I said to no one, hoisting the laundry bag higher on my shoulder as I made my way down the icy street.

I flung open the door of the laundromat and walked inside. The floor was dirty and slippery, stained where countless pairs of sludge-covered boots had dragged in the street salt, but it was warm inside, so warm I felt lightheaded. I walked to the far back of the place, past the tired young mothers holding bags of toddler-stained clothes and the clueless college guys putting their reds in with their whites and chose the machine closest to the wall, dumping the entire contents of my bag before realizing I had forgotten detergent.

Fuck. Detergent.

I closed the lid, feeling weak and exhausted. The skin around my eyes prickled as I stood there and my body continued to thaw, baking slowly beneath the sticky yellow light. I balled up the trash bag and stuffed it in my pocket, then turned back toward the door.

"Vodka gimlet, please."

The bartender nodded, took the cash and poured a double shot of Stoli into a cloudy rocks glass before topping it off with a squeeze of lime. I don't remember a time when my preference was anything other than vodka gimlets, though I don't know why I like them so much. It's just vodka and lime juice, nothing special, but I have a feeling it's something about the name. Gimlet. Like a combination of some word and *starlet*, maybe. Like a word you should aspire to be.

There was a boy with short, spiky blonde hair sitting at the bar a few feet away from me, nursing the dregs of a beer. He looked tough and, by the way his shoulders curved beneath the sleeves of his leather jacket, incredibly muscular, maybe in the way that meant he took steroids. He was alone, as far as I could tell, his face trained up toward the TV that was playing some football game above the bar. I eased onto the stool next to him.

"Hey."

Immediately I noticed he was Russian. He had an architectural jaw, the smooth-shaven skin pulled tight over its geometry, eyes clear and sharp, the light chemical blue of chlorinated pools. Maybe he had cried once, when he was younger and didn't know any better, before his father slapped him hard and told him he wouldn't have raised a weak son. He looked me up and down and gave a small smile.

"*Privet.*"

Of course. He didn't speak English. I'd seen a lot of foreign students come through there – the bar was near campus and sold good vodka cheap – but everyone I'd ever spoken to seemed to know at least a little bit. My Russian, the embarrassingly small amount I remembered from my time with Sloan, wasn't worth the effort. Or maybe he did speak and just didn't feel like speaking. I shrugged and raised my glass.

"Want a drink?"

"*Konechno,*" he said, breaking into a grin. I signaled to the bartender and he scooted his stool over to make room for mine.

It was raining when we left the bar so we stood under the awning of a bodega for a while. Fat raindrops dripped onto his stiff-gelled spikes of hair, which somehow managed to retain their structure. He lit his Zippo against the denim on his thigh. Even though I had matches, he insisted on lighting my cigarettes.

"*Kuda idyom?*"

I waved my hand vaguely forward, indicating neither direction nor uncertainty.

"I don't know," I said. "That way?"

He grabbed my hand and gave it a firm tug.

"Okay."

We took off in the direction of the subway, careening through the turnstiles like drunk teenagers.

When we got to my place I went straight to the bathroom, saying I had to pee, and got in the shower and shaved my snatch. It had been a while since I'd been with anyone and I had no idea how boys liked snatches nowadays. Landing strip? Bare? Trimmed into some sort of shape? Dense and wiry, like tangled fishing line?

I'd always thought there was something violently identifying about pubic hair, something so organic, so raw about it that was person-specific, the way it grew wild and insistent, held your shape and your scent, transforming the anonymous skin underneath that was skin like any other into something matchless and guarded, making it so you could only entrust it to someone who was between your legs selflessly, who wanted your pussy specifically because it was yours. I pawed at it with the dull razor, pulling my stomach into a concave C-curve as I doubled over to check for spots I might have missed.

How drunk was he? I was worried, worried how I would look to this stranger. But I was drunk and so was he and I didn't know him, so what did it matter? There was only so much he'd be able to see. I stepped out of the shower, dried myself off and replaced my clothes, then walked out of the bathroom, tossing the used razor in the trash.

He kissed me hard on the mouth, warm and wet, held my face in his hands with such an affected tenderness, the kind of fake thing people do when they want you to think what they're doing is meaningful, but his hands were too sweaty, too soft and fleshy and with none of the hardness I'd come to expect from men. I let the electric current drain from my body and sagged onto him, allowing him to push me into shapes. I was formless, I could move anywhere. He was tented above me, supporting himself on his swollen arms. My pants were bunched down around my ankles. I tried unsuccessfully to kick them off.

A drip of sweat fell off a spike of his gelled hair into my open eye and seared it shut. I felt faint. The siren hum rang out in the back of my skull and my stomach sucked into itself as I felt a wave of wet heat spread throughout my abdomen, gel-sweat and cum corroding the inflamed skins of eyelid and cunt. The red digits of the clock went charcoal ash and white and I was on the carpet listening to Tim Buckley, picking rust shavings off the fire escape; back home in my sleepy neighborhood, watching kids in grubby pastels run through the garden hose sprinklers; I was in Washington Square Park after the rain, squinting my eyes against the raw blue of the sky and breathing in the smell of worms.

I opened my eyes to feel the slow prickle of settling flesh. My temples throbbed lightly. I stretched across the length of the couch and exhaled, feeling the wave of new oxygen kick my blood into coursing.

The blonde boy was snoring next to me, his boxers and pants half on, shoes unlaced on his feet like he had made an attempt to leave but collapsed midway through. I peeled myself up and reassembled my clothes.

My body looked blue in the melancholy daylight, equal parts ethereal and run-through, Cimabue's Madonna. The cool-eyed blue of a holy streetwalker taking off her wig after a long night, russet, blonde, whatever color the john preferred, not the half-trusting Pretty Woman with the apple pie smile but a *beat* woman, a Beat Madonna, howling Courtney on her knees dripping manifestos and mascara, underworld saint-girl and her web of synthetics between the world and those threads of blue veins. All the holy women were blue.

I shook the boy's shoulder gently. He opened a sleepy eye.

"I have to go," I said. "Sorry. My laundry."

The heat rises off the asphalt in S-curves, blurring the street with shimmering mist. Tiny souvenir shops with vulgar beach t-shirts and dusty shot glasses every few feet. Bored men sit behind crackly cash registers reading month-old newspapers, glancing up every so often to accept fistfuls of cash from low-breasted women in sarongs. There are signs that apologize for not accepting credit cards, which everyone neglects to read. Outdoor fans spray thin bursts of mist onto the crowded patio.

I wipe the sweat from my forehead and under my arms, willing the droplets to evaporate but there is no wind. The air doesn't move here. I wipe it on my shirt. Even though I have sunglasses on they might as well not be there, the sun in my eyes as if it were trying to burn them out. I finish the caipirinha, stand up and think about what to do. There's an art gallery on the corner. I leave some cash on the table and go toward it, hoping for real air conditioning and a break from the murderous light.

Inside is damp dark. A woman sits at a desk in the corner. She's older, maybe in her sixties, skin smooth and tough like the good kind of leather. She wears lime green eyeshadow and bleeding crimson lipstick and her white-blonde hair with the black roots showing is pulled up in a falling bun, exposing her defined neck, the years around it like a tree's rings. I smile at her and walk deeper into the gallery.

The next room is full of bad paintings of African women. Women walking, holding children, holding fruit, topless with their breasts swinging. Women with strong collarbones and impenetrable expressions, long arms and fingers hanging down by their sides. I walk further, positioning myself beneath the ceiling fan, pull my hair off my back and shoulders to let in the breeze. The sunlight feels trapped beneath my skin, expanding inside me. The deeper I go in the gallery the larger and darker the paintings become, floor to ceiling canvases swathed in heavy charcoals and green-blacks, deep burnt reds.

In the back is a small door leading into what I assume is an alley. I step through it into an overgrown garden inside a square courtyard with high walls. Plants and flowers all over in total abandon, as if they'd taken root there of their own accord. A cracked blackboard with a faded menu covered by moss and ivy, broken filigreed metal chairs and buckets and watering jugs dumped long ago by someone in a hurry. I look up to see a huge mosquito bouncing along the length of the ivy-roped wall. The air is stiller.

I walk back to the front of the gallery and sit down opposite the woman, who hasn't moved except to open and close a notebook. I notice her teeth are incredibly large. Like horse teeth, but white. Blue white. She talks to me and I watch her. She tells me about her activism, how she used to be an artist before she moved here, how she organized a revolution among her students, about her high school dropout son. I imagine her going out into the garden at night, lowering down into one of the metal chairs and crossing one thin leg over the other, gazing up at the pinpricks of stars through the little box made by the tall walls. It's been so long since anyone's listened. Most people don't hear to listen. She doesn't ask me what I'm doing.

If no one does anything, then nothing gets done, you know?

I nod. Yes. I take one of her business cards and promise to visit again before I go.

Back in the heat I feel dazed. My skin burns with renewed fervor. Passing tourists take pictures of themselves in the street, of each other, of themselves again, not seeing the thing they're trying to see because they're always in its way. The sun is in my eyes again and everything dissolves beneath it like sugar in a hot spoon. I turn and head back in the direction of the gallery.

The woman is sitting at her desk exactly where I'd left her. I go to the chair I'd just gotten up from and sit down in it. She looks up from her notebook, penciled eyebrows rippling into two perfect waves.

Can I help you?

I stare into her green-rimmed eyes and see only ivy.

I'm sitting at my usual table, the tiny one that tilts, in the back just before the risers. It's always a little too dark to read or write but I come here because the laptop people don't. The only glow in the back is the Christmas lights, the fat glass ones strung up around the ceiling, red and blue and one or two purple, the colors that aren't out. The coffee is cheap and good and they always play the right music, Jeff Buckley and Neil Young and The Doors so far today. The little square table has one too short leg so I have to hold it down with my elbow and be careful moving so it doesn't pop up when I stand and spill wine all over my notebook, already twice its weight with the mystery liquids that have spilled and dried. The house wine is a heavy red that they serve in rocks glasses. The table is the perfect size to fit a glass of wine and a notebook and even though it probably isn't, I hope this is something they thought about when they designed it, or when they went picking things off the curb to furnish the Cake Shop.

Sometimes I sit here drinking and scribbling what I used to imagine were poems. Maybe they are poems, but I'm not completely sure what it takes for something to be a poem and if I don't think it's a poem, as the scribbler, then it seems unreasonable for anyone else to think so. Besides that, I don't think I'm capable of writing a poem. The word *poem* has a weight to it I shrink from.

Americaine! Why do you not honor your poets?

Is what the French woman asks Patti Smith at Jim Morrison's grave.

Je ne sais pas, madame.

Je ne suis pas.

Maybe *poet* is the word I shrink from.

I find myself at Cubbyhole often. It's a desolate crazy place, cramped and sticky with rainbow paper nightmares dangling from the ceiling and a jukebox that always seemed to play whatever it wanted. Most of the time it was in the mood for Whitney Houston. It's one of the only exclusively lesbian bars in the city, or at least it was once, before someone had the idea of putting it in the nightlife listings and now every tourist passing through the West Village comes in for a watered-down drink, along with every sparkle-eyed straight couple looking for a third. The great thing about it though is that it's always full of temporary people, and it's cash only so you don't have to hang around waiting to close a tab long after you're ready to leave. Everything about being there is fast but contained, like a whirlpool hot tub. I never go with the intention of meeting anyone necessarily, just to be warmed by the presence of other people. Alone, just a glass of wine and my notebook, it makes me feel good to know that the people around me are getting somewhere with each other. Blizzard, hailstorm or rainy Monday, someone from somewhere has made it a goal to get drunk and hook up or commandeer the jukebox, and the way that feels, like sitting still in a bucket of time watching the rest of it crash forward, is more comfortable than anything. Here is the world unfurling, indifferent to your input but carrying you along nonetheless.

This particular Monday I showed up straight from work wearing falling-off jeans and the ripped black hoodie with the thumb holes I'd had since high school, hair a tangled mess, smelling very attractively of Newports and burnt coffee. The bags under my eyes were what suggested my age. It had never occurred to me to change my wardrobe since high school. Same collection of shitty hoodies screenprinted with heavy metal bands, jeans cut way too low to be on trend, a thin iron cross necklace that looked like it had just escaped a life sentence at the Renaissance fair. Everything was either black or used to be so it all went together, and whatever kept fitting I kept wearing, until it either got lost somewhere or fell apart. Anyway, it was Monday, a snow-slush mixture coating the sidewalks, the gutters, but I had trouble even wedging myself between bodies to get to the bar, it was that packed. I poured myself into the space between two ladies in slacks (Midtown?), a ponytailed brunette in a tight orange polo (Jersey) and the loud blonde Australian who was a permanent fixture. Everyone needed to get warm that night.

The first thing you have to do at Cubby is put a drink in your hand. If you walk in there and don't make a move to get one within the first five minutes you end up looking either stood up or cruising. It's just a thing. Everyone is always checking out everyone in our tiny snowglobe world. You can't stand around too long checking your phone either because even if you are talking to someone it's obvious you're just doing it to avoid looking alone and small. But, plaster yourself right up against the bar and you've officially carved out a hole in the most coveted space. There are going to be endless arms reaching for drinks in between yours and for change over your shoulders but as far as anyone is concerned, you're established. You're rooted. Now stay.

Eventually the bartender, one of the tall weeknight guys with the Slavic features, turned his attention to me and let me order a vodka soda. I wanted a gimlet but they would've made it with Rose's lime, which is horrible. I didn't have the guts to ask for it to be made the proper way. Cubby bartenders don't have time for fancy drinks. I sipped and thought about what to do next. I wished I could go home, that I could work up the energy to do that, that it weren't so cold and I could afford a cab or had something on my feet besides soggy Chucks. I could feel the sickness flaring up in my throat in small pockets of heat, lymph nodes swelling tighter with every swallow. Gulp. I'd be there for a while. Shit.

It's gotten to the point of ritual, sitting in bars until the close, until four. Four the blessed hour. Two is when most bars that are not New York bars close, when it's still official night, but four is not that. If you haven't gone home by two you have to stay until four. Three, as everyone knows, is the death hour, when the breathing is shallow, the blood at low tide. The veins engorge, floating dangerously close to the surface, more susceptible than ever to the stirrings of the world. At three a.m. you feel the world's respirations whether you're awake or not. Asleep is when the soul opens, makes you extrasensitive, attuned to the breath. Awake you're exactly the same, but reckless.

But four, there's a holiness about four. The sky has that diluted indigo blackness, not the inky impenetrable black but the watercolor liquid black that marks the soft shift between night and day, that kicks the cycle into rotation again. When I leave the bar at four I walk around a bit to take the danger bite off the alcohol, then sit down someplace with my notebook, scribbling incomprehensible crazy until the breaking violet, or reading forward and forward in a book, none of which my conscious state will retain but whose energy, whose meaning I hope will filter down into the bottom of my consciousness and crack me open so the light can seep through. There's probably no way this works but I've been trying to make a practice of it, openness.

I looked up from my drink to see a girl standing in front of me, with wire-rimmed glasses and medium length curly hair. I don't know why but she had a cheesemonger's daughter sort of quality about her, like maybe in a different life her father owned a cheese shop and she stood behind his elbow and watched him double-cream the brie, sneaking small fingerfuls when his back was turned. Something secretly bad behind the tame features. Naughty, if naughty didn't have that weird sexual connotation. You don't see that often. I said hello.

"My friend and I have a bet," she said, pointing him out at the other end of the bar. "Are you here with someone or waiting for someone?"

"Neither," I said. "You're both wrong. What do I win?"

She laughed. Her purple V-neck shifted and I could see the beginning of a script tattoo peek out over her left breast, a curlicued name that started with M.

"I'm Chantelle." She extended her hand, soft chubby fingers. "I've never seen you here before."

"I'm never really here."

The girl I had been throwing glances at out of the corner of my eye on and off the whole time was now deep in conversation with a new one who'd just appeared, a tall brunette with long dreads and very straight, white teeth. I felt myself grimace.

"What do you do?"

"I don't want to say," she said. "Most people I tell walk away immediately."

"Now I have to know."

I ran through the possibilities. Porn star? Edible Arrangements artist? Neither of those were professions I would ever walk away from, and I told her so.

She laughed. "No, I'm a therapist."

I told her I didn't know what kind of person would turn down a therapist, in fact they should be so lucky to get to know one. I didn't tell her I sort of got why. Most people only want someone to know them as far as they'll allow. That old familiar fear that they'll pull something out from under you, sketch you better than you can sketch you, worse if you can't draw. Like a magician no one asked for manifesting quarters from behind your ears. The fear of being categorized, pinned down, explained is very real.

"Well?"

"Well what?"

"What about you?"

"Oh."

I took a long sip, trying to come up with an answer. There was no good one. The truth was not an option. People in bars lose their shit when you tell them you work in a sex shop. As if it's never occurred to them that sex is as much a business as any. That the physical realm operates on more than luck and a smile. When you tell anyone you work in a sex shop you immediately get that much more attractive to them, or that much less. A bad thing either way. I went with my standby false response.

"I'm a writer."

Which can have one of several outcomes. Usually it's a pretty safe choice because people don't know what to do with *writer*. They will either ask what sorts of things you write or they will say no, but what do you *do* – at which point you can tell them you're also a barista stripper dogwalker electrician and make them feel bad for insinuating that writing doesn't pay. Unless the other person is an actual writer, or an actual reader, the conversation is guaranteed to be short.

"Cool!" she said. "So what do you write? I'm reading *Fifty Shades of Grey* right now. Have you read that? It's crazy."

Or they will tell you what they're reading, which, if it's crap, won't upset you too deeply because you just lied about being a writer so what do you care.

"No, but if you like that sort of thing you should read *Carrie's Story*. By Molly Weatherfield. It's like the original *Fifty Shades* except written better and with real BDSM. It'll make you think about moving to California and becoming a professional pony girl, if you weren't thinking about it already. And if you haven't read the classics yet you should read those. *The Story of O* is basically the *Moby-Dick* of erotica.

Read de Sade too. He'll probably make you throw up but he was a luminary. Just try him on an empty stomach. And Sacher-Masoch. They're like the founding fathers of the whole thing. That's how S&M got its name, fun fact."

She goggled at me.

Chantelle remained attached to me for the rest of the night. Every time I went out for a cigarette I hoped she wouldn't follow, but once it sunk in that I really was alone she wouldn't leave my side. At one point she started trying. I felt the dial switch from casual flirtation to Operation Fuck. She kept dropping hints about how great she was in bed, how sexually adventurous, how she and her ex-girlfriend (*ex*-girlfriend) had split due to sexual incompatibility. I was glad I hadn't mentioned the sex shop. I kept drinking. I didn't know what to do with myself. The girl I'd been watching before was no longer talking to the girl with dreads. Instead there was another one, tall and lanky and gazelle-like, dancing by herself to whatever the jukebox was belching out. She looked like a wild colonial boy, hair in a shaggy brown mop that bounced around her head, like if you tried to hold her she'd slip right through your fingers. Her eyes were bloodshot to pieces. The girl I was watching was short, shorter than me, with a build like Sloan's but harder, leaner, her arms roped with muscles that made her tattoos ripple when they twitched. She was covered in them, all black and grey and doodles and linework, like an architect's sketchpad. Some of them were coordinates, outlines of maps, outlines of horses, trains, sharks. Piratesque. She looked like the world. She had an easy smile and a cute upturned nose and her close-cropped hair seemed to be going in places. I wondered if she got enough iron in her diet, biotin. Maybe it was genetic. Her face was red, maybe red like drunk but mostly red like outside all the time without sunscreen, who had the time, especially if everything is immediate and must be hurled into face-first if it's worth being experienced at all. All this coming off of her across four meters. Her movements were razor-sharp and urgent in the way that meant she was on coke. I felt like asking for some but then I remembered New York cocaine was shitty. It was the one thing the Midwest did better, upper drugs. That shouldn't make sense but it does. There isn't a whole lot there to perfect and everyone's bored.

I wanted to talk to her but I knew I looked like shit. She had so many girls around her now it wouldn't be an easy go. It was that smile.

This crazy energy that rippled out of her in waves. I perched my ass on a stool and tried to sip my drink in a cool way even though I could feel I was wobbly. Chantelle was ensconced in the bathroom line and it didn't look like she was going to be making progress any time soon. One of the bathrooms, the extra tiny one designed with the halfhearted goal of being the men's, was occupied by a couple that had been in there for the past fifteen minutes. I wondered if one of the girls was having a hard time coming because she was stressed out about the line, or because the bathroom smelled like shit. Probably it was both. I didn't understand why people still did this, fucked in public bathrooms. What is sexy about that. Bar bathrooms, airplane bathrooms, tiny cubes on a timer that smell like concentrated despair. Maybe it has to do with getting off on being selfish and inconveniencing people, I don't know. It can't be because it's taboo anymore. Maybe it was at some point in time – imagine the first couple in history, panting red-faced over some hole in an outhouse – but now it's about as taboo as a spit-soaked finger in the asshole. Cute when people think so.

I focused my eyes and saw the girl was looking at me. Holy fuck. I tried to adjust my molecules into a semblance of comfort and coolness but I had no idea what they were doing. For all I knew my eyebrows were traveling off my face. I was wasted. Did I need to put lipstick on? No, right? Lipstick was uninviting, it dissuaded people from kissing you because they had the inevitable smears of color to consider, and if they were unsure about kissing you to begin with that inevitability would push them toward no. Smooth, innocuously tempting lips seemed to be the cultural consensus. Either way it didn't look like I was going to get very far with mine. My lips were swollen and crackly dry like two lumps of cheap bubble gum, a rough wind-chapped armor, teeth underneath nicotine-stained and serrated like a fence in the dark. A blessing you couldn't see that in bar light. I tried not to smile with my teeth if I could help it.

I had only tried to whiten my teeth one time, with those weird waxy strips, but stopped after that attempt because the thought of wrapping my teeth in plastic every day for a month made me feel ridiculous, and anyway I knew I didn't have it in me, perfect white teeth. I was descended from a line of people who were traditionally lax about their teeth, didn't always brush them, ended up calcium deficient from diets rich in alcohol and salt and starch, destroyed them by default with unfiltered cigarettes and too many dark liquids, smoky teas and black fruit liqueurs and coffee strong as hell. Enamel-removing poisons. Our teeth were not made for the afternoon sunshine and grinning photograph smiles. They were teeth made for winter. For lack. Gnashing through tough things until they gave up and fell out. If the American Dream had a face it was white teeth. Veneer, shellac, paint over, white out. For this questionably toxic chemical at just $19.99, you too can look like you've never chewed a day in your life.

The girl was walking over. Through my wavy vision it looked like the crowd parted before her, bodies moved aside by the aura preceding her step. She planted herself in front of me. I could see Chantelle in the distance, having just exited the bathroom. She shot me a sharp look. I turned away from her and looked into the eyes in front of mine. They looked down into my hand.

"That was full when I went in there. You okay?"

"You're watching me drink?"

"You're watching me drink."

She looked at me and I realized I had no idea what color her eyes were. Translucent blue or green or that odd conflux of gold and moss called hazel. Whether they had a gray tint or deepened into turquoise or what. I couldn't name it. But it didn't matter. I don't think when you look in someone's eyes the objective is to see color.

It was the most important thing in the world, however, to know her name.

She put her hand on my thigh to steady herself. Her breath rippled the wisps of hair that had escaped from my topknot, spiraling down like thin black snakes.

"Morgan," she said. "How about I get you one more."

Morgan Morgan Morgan Morgan.

It's the last legible thing in the notebook before a stream of sideways subway slant and a series of dark splotches on the paper. It looks like watery mud, or trash juice, but it can't be. If I had dropped the whole thing in the street it would've soaked through the rest of the pages. Maybe just anonymous bar sludge, water sweating down glasses mixed with spilled drinks and lemon juice and everyone's street dirt carried in on their hands, on their sleeves. There was always the chance it was vomit, mine or someone else's, you can never be sure. The breeze blowing in through the window cracked open onto St. Mark's rustles the pages, crinkly and stiff where the mystery liquid had spilled and dried, strange warm winter day. The cheap white wine sits in its little mason jar, thin and acidic, carrying faint notes of dish soap and steramine from the badly rinsed glass. The fire escapes are dusted powdery orange with rust, mottled light and dark like saffron pollen on skin.

Morgan. The blood warmth had emanated from her like syrup. I had gone home with her as the three a.m. meta-dark eased into cold lavender morning, to her tiny icehouse room on Avenue B that she shared with a friend across a makeshift partition. We were neighbors, I remember finding that funny. Morgan there and me on my falling-down couch on Avenue C and Leigh in her basement on 5th, I wondered if Nik was still around, all of us so planetary close but separate and unfamiliar. In another life we would've all been friends I like to think, going places together, to readings and parties, going up in flames on each other's rooftops with drugs and music, necessary close, but that wasn't the life we had built for us now. Now we all came individually sealed with digital passcodes and our industrial strength wrappings were difficult to open. We reached out to each other with hands and mouths when we had the need, when we just wanted to get warm for a second before zipping back up into our respective worlds and slipping out into the larger one on a film of black ice.

Morgan didn't want me to use my mouth. My hand was what she wanted, but not inside. She held it tightly in hers on the walk home then shoved it beneath the waistband of her briefs, arched her neck high as my fingers moved over her in circles, came hard and quickly and then removed it, all business. She wanted to get herself out of the way so she could go to work on me. The way she touched me was how

I imagine a sculptor handles metal or clay, exact and methodical but with a love for the medium. No machinery there. I hadn't shaved and that was fine, it was supposed to look like this. What a thing to ever care about, how you looked. Who needed to look like anything when all you had to do was be. Morgan wasn't interested in looking at me. We were meditative and closed-eyed, perfect strangers, strange and perfect, content to leave the shapes ambiguous behind the screen. I softened beneath her and breathed even, full cycles until the final exhale and she fell away from me, released her fingers and I was empty again. She curled into my shoulder and let me sleep. I woke up clear to a note on the bed, her number scribbled on the inside of my arm in black Sharpie.

Yuppie guy in seersucker – is that what that is? – doubles back to consider the happy hour sign on the sidewalk, isn't swayed by the deal and keeps walking, white earbuds jammed tight between snug and tragus. I wonder what he's listening to. He looks like the type who would like Foxygen. No, not Foxygen. Maybe something classic like Bob Dylan. Not Bob Dylan. Something calming and lovely. Feist? Maybe he felt nostalgic for Bowie. I feel my hand cramping around the pen, the soft fleshy part by the thumb erupting in spasms every so often, and wonder what's going on. Pinched nerve? Carpal tunnel? Early onset arthritis? Probably not, probably it was just sore, but what kind of medical term does it make sense to use for sore. I swallow some wine. The front of my neck feels sore too. Mumps? A sore neck was one of the first symptoms. I had been vaccinated but I read that you could still get it even if you were. Of course it's like that. You never know what nightmare is going to flare up inside of you, and why. Looking it up on the internet is no help. Your chronic headache, it's probably dehydration but it could also be cancer. Good luck figuring it out.

Still, medical terms give you answers, even if they're not the right ones. In high school I stopped having sex with my boyfriend because it hurt too much. The first time we did it I think it hurt the normal amount. When he pushed himself into me it was this horrible searing pain, splitting but more than that, and I clung onto his shoulders with both arms as the tears ran down my face behind where he could see. I didn't want him to see me crying because then he would think it was his fault, like he was the one doing something wrong, like it was him specifically hurting me and not the situation itself that was painful. We tried a couple more times later and it was just as bad. I explained this to the OB/GYN, tears blossoming, as she calmly worked in a plastic speculum coated in gooey surgical lube. *Vaginismus,* she said after. Blinding, life-sucking pain upon insertion of object into vagina.

I was disappointed. It was not a fearsome term, more fitting instead to some geographically important land bridge. Vagin Isthmus. Connecting my body to his body. A passage. A rite of passage. Ugh. I wasn't convinced this is what I had, because sometimes I would try with my fingers and after a slow start and a series of gentle escalations I would feel myself warm up, open, tent. So I knew I wasn't incapable. My body didn't have its own icy agenda, it just needed a minute.

Vaginismus, I told him somberly anyway, with a stack of printed pages from WebMD. *I'm really sorry.*

I drink the wine and stare at the street. There's a little bookcase sitting by the trash heap, part of the trash heap, leaning against the bags spilling their colorful insides. The first week I moved here, I happily outfitted my entire living room with trash. My roommate didn't ask me where I'd gotten the stuff and I didn't tell him, what for. Broken full-length mirror, flipped upside down so the cracked part wouldn't obstruct my view, four-paneled Japanese folding screen, dark wooden dresser with two missing drawers. All this offered up by the world. I was thrilled. I couldn't imagine ever buying furniture in a place like this. I couldn't imagine doing this now. Now there was no way that bookcase didn't have bedbugs. Now is having to be one step ahead of everything because if you go the speed of anything it'll sideswipe you right into the fucking ditch. Now is don't touch that don't go there alone don't look at him especially not in the eyes, always have your boots on in case you have to run. Because the one time you don't is the one time you will. (I worry about the *Sex and the City* girls.) The fantasy of the magical life drowned in a puddle of sidewalk spit. Don't tempt disaster. You don't get a medal for succeeding as much as you do for fucking up less than you possibly could. Also what the fuck medal and who the fuck are you. Who the fuck. Are you. Someone is always asking, who are you. Are you? Knock knock.

"Miss, spare a dollar?"

I look down to see a traveling punk kid under the window, huge dirty backpack and pants made entirely of holes, shaking like a whippet. A steady stream of snot ran down his philtrum onto his lips, bloody where he'd chewed them. I look at my wine. Last dollar there. I shake my head and ease the window open some more, hand him the mason jar.

The books are heavy, bound in red leather, you left those for me as well. Przygody Dobrego Wojaka Szwejka. The Adventures of the Good Soldier Švejk. As far as I know they're the only books you ever read all the way through, and as far as I knew your whole philosophy was based on them.

I tried to read them when I was younger but my Polish wasn't good enough, I was clumsy with the words, stumbling over them, feeling my way blindly through each difficult one only to lose its meaning by the end, finally establishing a flow but reading without comprehension, words on top of words flying past with the pages, nothing happening. It was frustrating and eventually I gave up.

I put the books under my pillow and slept rectangularly for a couple of weeks, to try to absorb the meaning somehow anyway.

Since moving to New York I've owned six copies of *Valencia,* but I keep losing them to girls.

The first and most important came from Bluestockings, a feminist activist bookstore coffeehouse hybrid, almost too good to be true. It's a place no one tries to kick you out of if you don't buy anything, so I end up there often. I met Stephanie Schroeder there once, and Michelle Tea. They both signed books for me. Unfortunately I sent my signed copy of *Valencia* to Canada when I was drunk one day. There was a girl there whose mind I was in love with, who wore waistcoats and read Hume and studied medieval German architecture and so I immediately pictured a beautiful future with her, drinking coffee and reading in bed in cold winter daylight under dark blue sheets. But all I really did was get rid of my only signed copy of *Valencia.* On top of that, I'm not sure she ever read it.

I never gave Leigh a copy of *Valencia,* or a copy of anything. Leigh sent me soup when I was sick and had answers to questions post office- and tax form-related, but whatever emotional situation she was in made her absent. *Drinks soon?* would be met with silence for days at a time while updates of her internet activity faithfully rolled in, all this made that much more insulting by the fact that she lived five blocks away. I didn't understand how she could research "humane mouse extraction" so quickly after I discovered Hans hopping around the spikes in the dishwasher and still never want to stay the night after sex. He was the closest thing we had to a pet.

Still, Leigh was my operative girlfriend, so when I found out a film adaptation of *Valencia* was going to run at the queer film festival, I bought two tickets immediately. It looked like a bunch of filmmakers had gotten together and dissected the entire novel so that each was responsible for rendering a chapter according to their own vision. Twenty-one chapters, twenty-one different Michelles. I couldn't believe my good fortune. In general my favorite books are the ones you can't make films out of, but the very idea of *Valencia* played out in all these iterations of race, gender, voice and physical material, united only by the story, felt massively important. The voice of a generation stepping aside in favor of the portrait. I felt like rereading the book in anticipation but at this point couldn't bring myself to buy a seventh copy. I resigned myself to trusting my memory.

The inside of the warehouse was a neural metropolis. Huge plush beanbag somas scattered all over, video canvas LCD screens all backlit black-lit like a beatific power grid, performance artists in all manner of body paint, their ropey muscles rippling under color in shades of sunrise. Sex-sweat in the ether, crimson-lit dark. I had gone in a black lace dress with a faux leather bodice I found for four dollars in a thrift store, coal-powdered eyes and hair still wet. Leigh wasn't there yet. I located the bar, paid three dollars for an evil-tasting vodka grapefruit and walked around the gallery. I didn't know anybody and didn't know what to do with myself. I stood in front of a tampon stuck to a board for about twenty minutes.

It was a tampon, stuck to a board. One of those old-school cylindrical ones, not the new kind with the wings that puff out to keep it in place but just the plain cotton tower that goes up and down. Just stuck there. There was not even blood on the tampon, or gravedirt, glitter or liquid latex. It was not pickled inside a mason jar or made into a heroin cotton. There was nothing at all going on with it. I thought of the tampon in a teacup Margaret brings to her remedial art class in *Ghost World*, but there was nothing here to suggest repressed femininity, or anything else. It was mounted on a piece of particle board, stained and moldy at the edges. No sign of a title.

Eventually Leigh showed up when I was starting to feel buoyant, at which point my vision was already beginning to swim. She fed me some more drinks, because every time she asked if I wanted one I said yes. Of course I want a drink, there will be times when there will be no drinks and you have to drink in anticipation of those times, and these drinks are so tiny, and so weak right, so yes I need six of them, and also where have you been? I wanted to ask her this last question for real but I supposed there was a reason she wasn't telling me, which meant I didn't want to know.

The enormous lounge area had the highest concentration of beanbags, tossed haywire all throughout the periphery, along with these white blood cell-looking fabric constructions stretched floor to ceiling that made the red-bathed space look like muscle interior. The beanbags were smothered in people, drunk rolling blissed out strung out twos and threes and fours suspended in various stages of ecstasy and disarray, kissing spooning laughing napping in their own fucked-up little eden. A knot of ache took root in the pit of my stomach. I felt too upright, too standing, all lines and hard angles, all out of place. The two girls directly in front of me were lost in a kiss so tender-sweet I thought at any moment they would simply collapse into each other, atoms shifting just so in an impossible flourish of quantum phenomena. I grabbed Leigh's hand and pulled her down on a beanbag with me. We kissed for a moment, distracted, as she shifted to try to get a decent balance on the awkward surface, her fingers dragging over the rubbery material of my bodice.

Valencia started and it was nothing like I'd pictured, and it was everything. Each scene was a whirl of light and color so magnificently weighted it was hard to fully process what you were looking at. I was at the point of drunk where everything became infused with this crazy life-force energy, prana gone electric, the scenes so comfortable and familiar it felt like I could reach through the screen and create a home inside of them, Michelle was me and I was all parts of Michelle. Michelle with choppy green hair underneath her whore's wig, throwing it in the corner before taking her friends out for margaritas. Michelle introduced to knife play, a virgin despite her experience, the swell of her fist disappearing inside a woman for the first time. Michelle spinning out, lights and bass and heartstop after one too many of something and not enough of something else, midnight calling for the Greyhound schedule and pulling last exit money from the toes of her boots. Vegetarian Michelle stuffing turkey in her mouth alone in the kitchen on Thanksgiving, vomiting bile-slick muscle into the toilet.

At some point during the Claymation scene, Leigh leaned over and said she didn't feel well and had to go home. I nodded, transfixed by the screen. The sheer number of artists who were connected enough to Michelle Tea's work to take it apart and make a goddamn movie, refashion her words into a creature of living color was so momentous, so immediate and disarming that I started to cry on the spot. I mean how fucking great, to be loved that much. I hoped I would one day be able to make something luminescent like that, life-giving like that, that I had something sleeping inside me with a similar capacity to lighten and solidify, that one day I would be asked to do an opening sequence to a film based on something I'd done that had made someone, a bunch of someones, feel less cosmically alone, the camera zooming in on my fingers like it did on Michelle's alternating up and down pink hearts, one on each knuckle, as she arranged the opening credits. It was hard to breathe I was so excited, that subterranean cooking feeling that perks up when you suddenly have DIRECTION and know you are

DOING SOMETHING and that something's about to HAPPEN and all you needed was that one crystal moment and now it's there, you can turn around and pick up right where things started to get sludgy, out of the hole where it got dark and you couldn't see the bottom, except now you have some answers, the key to the poem, that light shining thing in the distance you couldn't find while searching but when you stopped straining your eyes you began to see clearly, hold onto it, everything's going to happen if you maintain your grip and keep coasting, if you can distill the calm shaking euphoria of having your present past and future selves all gathered up in your hands like night-blooming flowers, you can move the credits around with your ink-stained fingers before a room full of angels if you stay lit up, stir an iota of the universe if you don't let the energy dissipate, hold onto the pearl handed to you along the line in the mad rush toward excellent danger, if you can always feel like this.

I had started to sweat. The little plastic cup I'd been gripping had flattened in my hand, empty, the remainder of an ice cube squeezing out near the top. I remembered Leigh saying something to me. I turned to face her but she was gone.

Valencia ended and everyone filed out of the theater after the extensive thank you speeches. Or maybe the speeches happened before the film started, I wasn't sure. But I was freshly alone and decided it would be reprehensible to call it a night right then, after everything. The festival had apparently been going on all week. There were people who had been floating around this infrared cave for days, venturing out only for drugs, snacks and cigarettes, underground angels practicing soul communion on the beanbags, closed-eyed in the courtyard catching rainwater in their mouths.

Which was where I decided to go. It was time for a smoke. I sat down on what I thought was a ledge of some sort but was actually the ramp of a truck. I sat there indeterminately, sipping the last drink I could afford with my money, so methanol-strong I couldn't take a proper swallow without a shudder, I mean real sterilizing fluid variety. Maybe that's how I managed to stay healthy and disease-free. Cheap vodka just killed everything inside me. I sat. I drank. I smoked. I smoked again. I was planning to quit when I moved here but changed my mind for practical reasons. Smoking is the savior of the directionless. It gives you a reason to hang around someplace you have exactly nothing to do in. A sense of purpose, even if that purpose is to cremate yourself from within.

I sat there with my cigarettes a while longer and thought about Michelle. About how badly she wanted Iris, and how badly she didn't want Iris, and how she just wanted to be wanted by Iris, and how ultimately she just wanted to hold onto herself. Iris the hypnotic pool that gave no water. There was an Iris in every eye.

I watched everyone. Friends and strangers and lovers exchanging lighters and kisses and phones. A girl with long brown hair and a smooth, pretty face sat down next to me. We talked about nothing. She bought me another drink. I lit her cigarettes for her.

In the morning I woke up next to her in one of the beanbags, dress pushed all the way up around my torso, tights and underwear bunched in a sad roll halfway down my ass. It looked like the girl had passed out from exhaustion while attempting to wrestle them off. Tights are difficult, I don't blame her. I located my phone next to her shoulder. Five a.m.

I scrolled through the unread texts, head heavy with metallic vapor. Nothing from Leigh, not even a *got home safe*. No *get home safe?* either. I blacked out the screen. I didn't know what sort of words I was expecting when it had always been clear that I didn't, and wouldn't, and would never move her. What are you supposed to do with words. In a language where "love" is for taking a bullet and also a particularly good piece of pizza, the best you can do is take aim and wish.

I peeled myself up from the beanbag, buried so deep it was almost an ab workout, and reassembled my clothes into a suggestion of propriety, picking up all the bits and pieces I had come with scattered around. The entire room was still asleep, comatose angels in twos and threes and fours strewn over the beanbags, each other, the floor. The audio portion of whatever performance piece was going on last night was still running on loop, some sort of S&M scene between two girls. *You like that, you like that you little whore? Look at me when I'm talking to you!* bouncing off the empty walls. I thanked the high heavens for protecting my belongings and the company of the night for not stealing anything, even though I had made it so damn easy. Queer people are generally not assholes, especially not to each other, but you never know what the universe is going to do. You make an offering and take a step back, and whatever meets you halfway is destiny.

The warehouse floor is vast, bigger than it was last night in the red light, an iron gray lake in the bright stillness. I take small, light steps to avoid waking anyone, a handful of condoms from the basket near the door just in case, and emerge at full height into the sunlight.

Another thing about airports: you can't really smoke cigarettes in them. You can, if you resign yourself to one of those mini crematoriums where you can hotbox with the rest of the desperate, but knowing what that looks like from the outside is almost enough to make you not do it. Beyond that, it doesn't feel good. It doesn't feel good because there's nowhere to breathe out.

This airport doesn't have a mini crematorium and I wonder how many people have missed their flights by taking the chance to go outside.

The guest speaker in Ms. Johnson's class, somebody's father, demonstrated how tar collects in your lungs with some viscous black liquid in a Coke bottle. He swirled it around and around, dark veins blooming up along the sides and snaking down in drippy rivulets. It wasn't supposed to look appetizing but it did a little bit, thick and syrupy like cola concentrate.

No liquid, healthy lungs.

Black liquid, sick.

We carry our deaths inside of us, sleeping. Rilke wrote that, more or less. They grow with us and mature, unfurl slow or rage awake. Like bones, like nerves, like anything formative, the scaffolding we hang the weight of our lives on. Separate but elemental. We make our deaths. Our deaths make us.

I found my brother's Marlboros on the nightstand that day after school. I remember feeling very curious about the black liquid. About being able to breathe a part of him in.

I never wanted to smoke, but quitting at this point would feel like betrayal.

In the picture a pink-cheeked baby sits fatly on the carpet, the beginnings of messy blonde waves pinned haphazard atop her head. An array of objects is laid out in front of her in a wide half-moon: spoon, stethoscope, pen, test tube, Bible. It's her first birthday. This is ritual.

My hand hovered over the stethoscope and I remember someone, maybe it was grandma, telling me that mom got all excited then, saying Oh we're going to have another doctor, and then someone else, I think it was you, saying Don't be so sure. My hand dropped back into the folds of my frilly white dress. A minute later I grabbed the pen and the camera flashed, but I haven't been able to find that picture.

Our mother chose the stethoscope immediately, at least that's what she tells me. You sat there forever, choosing nothing until she got tired of watching you and removed the things. Our father chose the Bible, but he didn't live that way.

This is how we read our destiny. It's foolproof until it isn't. She told me I wouldn't let go of the pen.

Journalist, she later urged. Teacher. Critic. Scribe.

After the insanity of Pride, the parade and the bars both made unbearable by the viscid heat, we found ourselves at a massive rooftop party on the edge of the city, the Empire State building a rainbow pinnacle over the shadowy streets. This particular party was full of kids on molly who appeared to be having sex on blankets in the middle of the roof. Mischa strained her eyes to confirm. A beautiful blond boy, so pale he glowed in the reflected light, was molded on top of the hard-drawn outline of a dark-haired boy, moving fluidly over him like a sine wave. They were definitely having sex.

She rolled her eyes, not sure what it was about seeing strangers fuck in public that was so irritating. Not that she was embarrassed by it, or embarrassed for the people involved. It was something about the display of sex in general. Unlike porn, which was work, which could be art, made for looking either way, this type of showiness seemed like a sophomoric act of rebellion. Out in the open but wrapped up in each other at the same time, as if to say, *We can create our own little universe right here if we want to, you and your lonely Bud Light can fuck right off.* A perfect example of couples' privilege in the world: solo masturbation is consistently a huge no-no, but masturbation with a partner seems intrinsically okay. Nothing like seeing two people so into each other they forget where they are and make you remember.

As she was making these observations the people on the blanket switched positions. The dark-haired boy now had his face submerged in the blond boy's ass. The blond boy arched his back, raising his butt cheeks higher to obscure the dark-haired boy's inexhaustibly swirling tongue.

Mischa looked down into her beer, neither disgusted nor jealous, and thought hard about what she was feeling, unwilling to accept that it could very well be nothing. Did she want to be fucking someone on the roof then and there? Did she wish she could be fucking Krista, who had gone home earlier in the day because she said she was tired? Pride made everyone tired, but there seemed to be something else beneath Krista's exhaustion. Something inside her eyes. They used to go on forever, she remembered, filled with dark warmth, all the liquidity of deep brown eyes that made you feel cradled inside them when they held your gaze, but at a certain point Mischa couldn't isolate on the timeline they had become flat and cancelled like a junkie's, parallel points of the void vanishing behind matte smoke screens. The way chocolate gets when you leave it out so long the powder particles emerge from the inside and cover it in hoary dust. Her eyes looked dehydrated.

Maybe she was imagining it. Maybe it was her own baseline paranoia, so useful in dealing with difficult situations. Maybe it was nothing and maybe it wasn't. But they hadn't always looked that way. Not during their first drink in college when Krista still had a boyfriend and flicked them up shyly, thick black lashes through honey-colored bangs. Not the summer Saturday in the record store when they glowed for a hidden Tim Buckley, the honor of being the first to introduce her new girlfriend to *Goodbye and Hello.* Not that night on the doorstep when they burned with half-fever after walking a mile in a snowstorm to bring Mischa wine. No, they hadn't always looked that way. Sickness always showed first in the eyes.

Mischa scanned her surroundings, full to capacity with colorful humans deep in ecstasy or conversation. I was off in the corner somewhere, talking to a lithe model covered head to toe in glittering body paint.

She leaned over the edge of the building and thought about the drop, about what it would feel like for her skull to smash over the pavement like a rotten gourd. Whether anything, besides the realities of physical disengagement, would feel different. Who would be called away from the festivities to come clean her body up, what the headlines would do with a Pride suicide, whether she would have to be scraped off the sidewalk, or hosed off. How with one small move she could ruin my entire weekend, possibly even damage me for life.

If this is sex, I've never had sex before, I thought, watching the boys fuck in the middle of the roof. I don't know where that line popped in from but suddenly it was the only one to describe the feeling I was having, that I was watching something sacred, on a different spiritual plane than anything I'd ever done. There were couples and groups scattered all over, tangled angels in twos and threes and fours in various stages of consumption, making room in their bodies to fit more of something inside, drinks and drugs and each other, pill to tongue to mouth to mouth, everyone so full of chemical love it gave you a contact high. The Garden of Nightly Delights in supersaturated real time.

But the boys were what had my attention. They looked unreal, running on their own strip of film under a heavenly beam from nowhere against the dark mass of bodies. The softness around their edges was what made me stop listening to the girl in front of me and look. Delicate swan pose of throat over shoulder, Adam's apple to clavicle to sternum to tongue, convex into concave seamless like the holy shroud –

How had they gotten there that night. Were they friends or boyfriends or strangers. Did it matter. Maybe it did and maybe it would but not now. Now was singular and separate with no connecting point but itself, and they would never recreate it, and it was beautiful.

I was drunk and that might've been why but I felt a tear run down my cheek.

Leigh. I told her I would wait for her, but I knew before I got there she wouldn't come. When someone says they'll try it's always a loose maybe. With Leigh even a yes meant there was a half chance it was no.

The dark-haired boy had climbed on top of the blond boy and was fucking him hard. I turned my focus back to the glitter girl but there was empty space where she had been. I wondered how long I had been standing there alone and looked around for Mischa, who had wandered off somewhere to get a drink a little while ago. I located her on the other side of the roof, leaning over the railing. I made my way over to her, taking care to step on the edge of the boys' blanket as I passed.

"Misch."

She turned to face me and her eyes were red like she'd been smoking or crying but I didn't smell pot. I put my arms around her.

"I'm here, Misch."

She sagged onto me with a weight I didn't realize her tiny body possessed, as if her soul had become waterlogged.

"Just look at this shit." I waved my hand at the circus on the roof.

"Pride."

"What's there to be proud of? We're all fucking lonely."

She laughed. I massaged her back, running my knuckles over the knobs of her vertebrae. God she was tiny. Was she eating. About as much as I was, probably. Shit. I put my hands on her shoulders.

"Let's get a fucking taco."

"I'm not hungry."

"Let's get a taco anyway."

"Wait." She glanced in the direction of the boys. The dark-haired boy was standing up now, pouring a load of cum into the blond boy's mouth.

"Would you ever fuck anyone on a roof?"

I twined my fingers through hers and smiled, tugging her toward the stairs.

"If it would make them feel better? Of course."

"But objectively, why wouldn't you? If you had the option to exist or not, and existing is such a fucking ordeal, what is the worst thing about not existing?"

Mischa and I were sitting in a corner of The Library, another holy place, under the watchful eyes of a madly drawn Lovecraft. We were comparing suicide resumes. She told me about the roof and the NyQuil and I told her about that day with the pills and the vodka and the blue sky, how I had gone out of my head for a moment and it was like waking up in a new body when I came to. Holding my mother tightly in the kitchen, infusing an apology into her when she didn't even know anything was wrong.

I don't know why I never killed myself, is what I ended up telling Misch. Not because I'm a good person. Not because I'm afraid of dying. *I guess I just want to see what happens next.*

Once the fact settled in that Krista was leaving, Mischa took off for the bathroom and tried to wash down an entire bottle of Xanax with a bottle of NyQuil. Krista banged on the door and convinced her to come out and she had to spit it all out in the sink, chastising herself for how stupid she was being. Too much NyQuil and she would've been That Girl, committing suicide in front of her ex-girlfriend to teach her a lesson. Mischa told me that it was always going to be an attractive idea, but all things considered she wouldn't try again.

"Are you kidding? Not existing is way scarier than existing. I don't know how good a person I've been, I'm not sure I can judge that, but I wouldn't want to risk ending up in *Gehonim* before I've had the chance to make anything right."

In Judaism, *Gehonim* was hell. It was what happened to your soul if you were a shitty person in life, but unlike the Christian version of hell, splatter-painted with all the demons and fire, you simply ceased to exist. No fire, film cut, blanked out, nothing left. I thought it sounded great. She shook her head.

"Think about it," she said. "You just don't exist. Think about how terrifying that is. Your soul doesn't end up in the light or the dark. It just gets extinguished. You're not in the good place, or the bad place, or the neutral place, because there's no place for you at all. You've disappointed God so much He doesn't even find it worthwhile to make you suffer. It's like you're beyond death, because you never lived. You're deader than dead. You're dead to God."

Then she added, "You would have to have done something

really bad for God to blot out a part of Himself."

I sipped my drink and sat with this, but I had trouble wrapping my head around why it was so bad. When I pictured hell it was this vast expanse of white space, nothing in front of me except the static silence, the silence on the inside of my skull. A permanent splinter of the mind. Consciousness on and nowhere to put it, left to spin around and around itself for whatever forever is. Forever aware of the nothing, like being pumped full of amphetamines and strapped to a chair. In light of that, not existing seemed wonderful. It would be exactly like going under. No thinking. No feeling. No pain.

"Well," I said, "What if people who remember you are still alive? Like family? If you never existed, what is it they remember?"

"You know about false memories."

"Does God implant false memories?"

"Now you're just being stupid."

I finished my drink, confirming the assessment.

"I don't know," I said. "I would rather not exist, I guess, than be in eternal anguish."

"Anguish takes many forms."

We sat like that for a while, on either side of the rickety table, tracing the carvings in the wood. She went outside for a cigarette. I finished her drink and ordered two more. Mischa with her enormous effusive heart.

I knew she'd close up if I tried to needle her more about it, but it bothered me that I couldn't see what she did. I didn't understand and didn't have to say it, but I didn't tell her I wanted to for the most selfish reason. For fear of being excluded by default. Separated from her by a shortness of belief. That if we both went to hell we'd end up in two different places.

I didn't tell Mischa I'm lying every time I explain why I'm still alive, *to see what happens next.* This is bullshit. Everyone has their public reason, and we tell each other all the time and sometimes we believe it. But it's not until someone asks you *why haven't you killed yourself* that you start to really get somewhere. The place you end up when all your escape routes are blocked.

Cross-legged on the dirty cream carpet, a pile of vinyl fanned out in front of me in a wide half-moon. The record player is one of those radio tape deck hybrids with what I thought were impressive speakers. I've always liked putting the records on, the little blip-scratch when the needle first touches vinyl, the saturated hush before it begins to spin. Like the world is suspended for a moment, has the capacity to be rewound.

The Clash's Combat Rock was my favorite. I used to dance to it in my tutu. Mom made me take ballet when I was little because she thought I had crooked legs. Sometimes I faked a sprained ankle so I'd be allowed to sit it out. I was very manipulative as a kid I think. But my legs aren't crooked anymore, so you can take that for what it's worth.

Anyway, The Clash was exciting. The record just felt like energy. As a nine-year-old I was very attached to them, though occasionally Pink Floyd and Tim Buckley made the rounds. You left them all for me when you left, and the record player radio tape deck hybrid. Said you didn't need them anymore.

Wszystko Twoje, you said. All yours now.

I spread out on my back and become still under the sound. Tim Buckley's "Phantasmagoria In Two." That song needs to be played on vinyl I've realized, the soul part is lost otherwise. The needle has to draw it out. The way it sounds like how rain feels, gets into you like that. The pure unyielding voice with its undercurrent of a wail threading itself through your fibers, becoming the glue that holds it all together, keeping you alive.

You should've listened to more Tim Buckley, I tell the ceiling.

God damn it.

Twice I got nowhere going forward so maybe I would try going back. I rub my temples where an ache has taken root, pressing hard on the delicate indents. I pick the book up again and go straight to the end, the pages of the last chapter stained black from the bled out ink of Sloan's inscription. For some reason it feels heavier this time.

It's incredible how all sorts of things can come out of a pair of pants, fuzz, watches, clippings, crumbly aspirins, you stick your hand in to pull out your handkerchief and you pull a dead rat out by the tail, things like that are perfectly possible.

Well he wasn't wrong. You never know what shards of the world you'll find in the things that go out to see it with you. In one of the purses I only use for special occasions I discovered a package of licorice along with an actual hammer and nails.

I unzip my purse and look inside. In addition to the underwear and necessities (ID, credit card, both zipped into the side pocket because I've lost too many wallets), I find one smashed cigarette, a tampon with a punctured wrapper and half a granola bar. The granola bar wrapper looks like it's been flapping off for ages, bits of tobacco and lint stuck to the nuts and dried fruit. No sign of my phone or keys. I wonder what time it is, how long I've actually been here, how many times Mischa has tried to call. I shove my hands into my jacket pockets. Lipstick and empty aspirin bottle in the left, pen and teabag in the right, and, thankfully, the keys. I replace the things inside their pockets and pull my jacket tighter around me. I look at the lint-and-tobacco granola bar.

How hungry was I?

They were definitely not shrooms.

Sloan's roommate held up the bag of weed sprinkled with grayish-white flecks.

"Shrooms," he said sagely, appraising our raised eyebrows. "This'll get us there."

I was nervous. Weed alone made me feel awful, sluggish and dim and fringe-paranoid, in a constant state of subtle nameless dread, that feeling of waking up half-conscious in a place you know you don't want to be but you're still too underwater to really grasp why. And now I had to smoke weed with shrooms in it. Add to that I didn't have a good relationship with hallucinogens. I didn't trust my head with them. Uppers, downers, the ones that operated on the right-to-left sliding scale, those were the drugs I could handle. Safe drugs. The ones that kept reality as I'd left it but only went so far as to inject it with light or dark. It was the other ones, the ones that pulled its skin off and turned on the fluorescents that were the trouble.

Having had no previous shroom experience, I took the thing at face value. How bad could it be? The flakes looked like Lilliputian sunflower seeds. It didn't occur to me at the time that they could have been anything, crack or PCP or Krokodil as far as I was concerned, that even small things take effect, that you had to be careful in a world where adding one more oxygen to a water molecule would kill you instead of quenching your thirst.

Sloan's roommate produced a marbled blue bowl from inside the glove compartment and stuffed it. I looked at Sloan.

"You don't have to do it if you don't want," she said, reaching for the bowl. "We'll still have fun."

But the idea of being sober around a bunch of high people at an amusement park seemed worse than being dangerously high, and I told her so.

"Okay then. Your turn."

I torched the tiny clump and inhaled. The smoke ballooned out through my lungs and it felt like it was singeing them, forcing its way into the tight places, burning fissures between cell walls.

Right away it was clear I'd done something I shouldn't have. This was exactly what happened when you fucked with the Ouija board and called up a demon. Ice drops of warning sweat pinpricked up my back. I made conscious note of the fact that I didn't feel anything.

Sometimes that worked with drugs: you convinced yourself you didn't have the fear, and then you just wouldn't get it. Everyone would think I got high along with them while I maintained my secret safe handle on reality. I crossed my fingers and concentrated on breathing, willing the thing to back down.

The minute we were out of the car the world fell off its hinges. Everything in my line of vision went tilt-shift and it felt like someone had undone my body's zipper, insides exposed to the atmosphere, blackening quickly like fresh radium. The sun was setting and the light on the horizon made it biohazard cinematic, a thick dusting of 2D iridescence sprinkled over the backdrop like technicolor snow.

We got in line to the entrance and it slowly began to register that I had to deal with other people. There was no way around it. Unfortunately I'd become incapable of moving my arms or tongue, and even if I could move my tongue it didn't matter because I'd forgotten how to speak. My tongue had plastered itself to the base of my mouth, devolved past language, slackening into a primordial rigidity behind the military rows of teeth. Good thing I had my sunglasses on. I couldn't begin to imagine what my eyes looked like. Sloan had her arm around me, trying to steady my pace as I muscled one foot in front of the other.

"We have to go to the bathroom," I said in what was hopefully a whisper, was hopefully what I really said, but it could've been anything. It was entirely possible the connective channel between my brain and mouth had snapped and my mouth was expelling something completely deranged. I prayed Sloan was enough on my wavelength to intuit what I wanted.

"What?"

"BATHROOM!"

Sloan squeezed my arm hard.

"Shh…be cool."

She locked her arm around my waist and steered me toward the restrooms at the entrance of the park. I clamped my mouth shut with as much force as I could summon. I was trying to swallow the fear but it was like a live squid wriggling its slimy body up my throat to escape.

Once inside, I headed straight for the back wall and collapsed against it. The entire world had gone blank and the air was so gas-thick and heavy it crushed me beneath it, spreading my body thin like rice paper. I felt Sloan but I couldn't feel her, stuck in the purgatorial white space from which there was no up or down. There was nothing else out there, nothing beyond, only this. This was home now, this everything that looked deceptively like it should look in real life but desaturated, blanked, drawn in colors made to cover, taupe, gray, off white, anonymous hospital waiting room, color of dirty rags, dishwater, the yellowing white of an empty room left to eat away at itself, my body going bloodless in it, sick white against the wall in a pair of unyielding arms. I trained my eyes on the linoleum tile and forced myself to understand it. It looked like chopped onions at first, then cracked yellow teeth.

"Do you see the teeth?"

"Baby…what teeth?"

The fact that she couldn't see them was so devastating I started to sob. She wasn't in here with me, no one could get in here. She held me tighter and in my vast despair tried to convince me that I would eventually be okay. *Uspokoysa*, she said in blood language, in an effort to get the words to reach me. *Calm down. They're just drugs.* Relax. Relax. Relax.

Something like an hour went by before I felt capable of standing up. Sloan wasn't swayed by the idea of living in the bathroom forever and pulled me up gently by the arm. I closed my eyes against her shoulder but I couldn't get the whiteness to go dark. There was only the white space, the blankness on the inside of my skull. The nothing had gotten in.

As I passed by the mirror I made the mistake of looking in it. The cardinal rule of drugs – you never look in the mirror unless you're ready to go deep down. My eyes were enormous, swollen with color, the whites an angry red shot through with bruise-colored supernovas. The fear had risen up through my nasal passage and spread itself thin along the optic nerve, threading behind my eyes to fill them with ink that flowered like fireworks. The darker they got the lighter everything else did until it was just them and the mirror, me and the white space, everything else fuzzed out.

This was hell, what I was seeing. Crushing nothingness and no exit from it, infinite immobility in an expanse of dead white. Bad craziness. Eventually Sloan succeeded in coaxing me out.

Once outside, the sunglasses resumed their post on my face. I took my cautious steps, allowing Sloan to lead me to new safety. It's funny how when we're the most unfit to be out in society we think if we just act cool no one will notice, but really that's when people notice the most. The characteristic hard set of the mouth, the expressionless face lines, the overly metered step. The attempt at equilibrium is so unbalanced it's hilarious.

Sloan deposited me on a bench and I sank into it, acknowledging my new surroundings. Okay. I was sitting there. I could relax. No one knew what my eyes looked like behind the shades. It would all be okay. I would just sit there, maybe forever, and everything would be okay.

"Maybe you should eat something?"

"Dippin' Dots."

The words escaped immediately. I had just been fixating on a kid nearby digging into a mountain of tiny pink and yellow spheres. Spheres, straightforward and self-contained, were reassuring and attractive. Something cold seemed like a good idea too. Tiny cold spheres were exactly what I needed.

"Okay," she said. "Will you be okay until I get back?"

Of course. Of course I would be okay. I could handle sitting on a bench. I could just close my eyes behind the screens and not engage with the world, ignore it completely, and maybe then it would stay on its own side of the fence and everything would be okay. I squeezed my eyes shut and opened them to a chubby girl standing in front of me checking her phone, her Daisy Dukes splayed open over damp floral bikini bottoms. Her cellulite moved in peach and cream waves, rippling serenely as she shifted her weight from one foot to the other. A gigantic black fly tried to make a home on her leg and she countered it with an aggressive smack, sending a tidal wave through the calm undulations.

"I'm fine," I said, maneuvering my mouth into a smile. "Please come back soon."

I put *Hopscotch* back in my bag and stretch out in the squeaky leather chair. The typeface is microscopic. It's not like I would even finish it by the time I got to Texas, and Sloan already knew I'd never read it, so what was the point of starting now? And those papery thin pages, translucent and dry like dead eyelids. You turn them and turn them and they just multiply like some sort of blinding Escheresque tessellation. The weight of it off my knee was a relief.

Now what?

I had finally sobered up from last night, from this morning, and what I felt from the sobriety was upsetting. The tips of my fingers were tingling and there was a bad pressure in the back of my throat, something taking root there I couldn't swallow no matter how hard I tried. I had no sleeping pills, no Xanax, no anything, and the minutes ticked on incessantly but didn't move anywhere at all.

I disentangle my limbs from the seat and head toward the first shiny countertop I see gleaming in the terminal.

"Where are you off to?" she asks, pouring the last sip of a warming beer in her mouth.

The girl looks like trouble, or maybe I want her to be. Thick dark hair, short and choppy and cavalier, one of those haircuts that meant she was a lesbian or just super fashiony. Her voice was low and gravelly but definitely sensual, definitely feminine, a thin sugar film over steel skeleton. I imagined she would be a good phone sex operator, the depth of that voice balancing out its edge. She looked like she was good at dealing with other people's fantasies. Like she could handle the strange.

"Austin," I say, taking a tentative sip of my drink. It was my sixth and it was still daylight. The girl had taken the stool next to me when she came in and watched me scribble on receipt paper for a couple minutes before speaking so I hoped I didn't appear drunk if she'd been cataloging my movements, but who cared? If you're going to be drunk anywhere you might as well be drunk in the airport, where you're under no obligation to be anything to anyone, least of all anything impressive.

"Cool. I'm going to Vegas."

I examined her. Her skin was pale and glowed in the way that meant she was healthy and her collarbones were sharp and raised, creating deep hollows. You could tell water stayed in them for at least a second when she came in from the rain. Eyes large and dark like wells. This girl could hold things.

"What are you going to Vegas for?"

"My friends are there," she said.

"Humping the American Dream?"

"What?"

"Hunting the American Dream?"

"Oh." She laughed. "Yeah, you could say that."

I imagine walking out of the terminal with this stranger. Just walking out together into the city that would look different since I left it and into a new life, fuck our checked bags. Well, fuck hers, I thought, remembering I had nothing.

"What are you going to Austin for?"

I finish my drink and crack an ice cube with my teeth.

"I'm not really sure."

"Maybe you should figure it out."

Her hand brushes my thigh on its way up to touch my arm. She's drunk too, or naturally luminescent, crimson orbs where before her cheeks were pale, large pupils infused with black glitter. How long has she been here, where was she really going. Vegas. Whose dream was she going to go chase there, American or otherwise. You always hear so much about the American Dream. What is that. Imagine any other country with its own trademarked dream. You emerge from the womb and the doctor slaps your ass and hands you a treasure map, ex marks the spot, now go get 'em, make us proud. A race before you even know how to aim your piss into the toilet, the starting whistle timed to go off at the exact moment you're pulling up your pants.

At some point I say all this in a way that makes no sense and the girl laughs. I'm not sure if the laugh indicates appreciation or absurdity but it's the same either way and I hope it's both. She asks if I'd like a shot and I nod. Yes. Of course I want a shot, there will be times when there will be no shots and you have to drink in anticipation of those times, and also where have you been all my life? I get the impulse to say that last bit for real but manage to stop myself before it falls out of my mouth.

Two shots of Stoli Vanil appear in rocks glasses, unusually generous for an airport, but also the bartender looks like the type of guy who would feel personally accomplished for watching two random girls make out. I pour it down. Stoli Vanil. Sloan and I used to drink it before marathon sex sessions because one of us once came to the realization that it had aphrodisiac properties (it does). The warmth that takes off inside me is full-bodied, gorgeous. The girl's hand finds its way to my left wrist, her slim fingers running up and down the main vein, waking it up.

The other advantage to falling in love with strangers is getting lost in the timeline. Strangers who look at each other That Way, this way, the way we were now looking at each other are always seeking to throw dirt over the hole someone else left, and that alone is a comfort. It's hard to imagine anyone wanting to voluntarily deal with the pressure of the first, which is why I only know how to deal with used people. I don't want anything untouched because if I take it and mistreat it my memory is forever there, not lost in a million other fingerprints, but *there*. When you're the first at anything you sign a covenant, make your imprint, carve your name into the wood. You can't blot it out. It always means so much more than it means, to be the first word, the first kiss, the first disappointment. You set the timer. Everything happens afterward because you were the ultimate cosmic *yes.*

Her nail polish is chipped black, raw skin shining pink beneath the exposed bits of nail. She runs her fingers down from my wrist to open palm and back up again and I watch them, hypnotized by the motion. Everything was contained in that back and forth. The largest wrist vein was elevated all the way to the surface, freshwater blue under the thin layer of skin.

She asks for my number. I tell her no because I'm on my way to convince someone to fall back in love with me, but under any other circumstances I would be thrilled to let her complicate my life.

"But there is something I can give you."

I reach into my bag and pull out the copy of *Hopscotch.*

"The perfect airport book," I say, getting up and slinging the bag over my shoulder.

Her eyes walk me out. I try to walk straighter, try not to stumble, will my body into looking graceful and classy and maybe making my hips swing a little bit. Unless she drinks much more I know she will remember me, if for nothing more than the curve of my ass and my veins under her fingers. I hope she makes it to Vegas and pins down her dream.

Coasting on the thin strip of sunlight on the airport floor, I get all the way back to my gate before realizing I had given away La Maga without even learning who she was.

"Whatever," Mischa said. "Let's do these drugs."

I was skeptical. Not that saying no to drugs is a habit, but it's almost inaccurate to call what we have here cocaine. That high school joke of selling bags of oregano as weed to middle schoolers, that's this, only with what seems to be lidocaine and Carpet Fresh. This shit is cut so aggressively that the only thing about it that feels like drugs is the numbness in the nasal cavity and the toxic sludge hangover from the chemical fillers. And not that I'm a goddamn scientist, but I'm pretty sure you shouldn't be able to fall asleep comfortably after several lines of blow.

This time we were outside Cubbyhole with a retired model who kept idly smoking some sort of foreign menthol 120s and a girl who could only be described as her keeper, a nervy-looking dyke who seemed like she deliberately eyed people on the street extremely close, to justify picking a fight with whoever she thought was looking at her wrong. For some reason Mischa had struck up a conversation with her while I was at the bar, and now thanks to her persuasive charm it looked like we were all going to do coke in the bathroom together.

Which was okay. I was just happy we didn't have to pay for it. I don't trust Mischa to buy drugs. I think she trusts too many people. Once she made us stand outside Monster Bar in the freezing cold for twenty minutes while she installed her contact information in the phone of a staggering drunk Bulgarian who insisted he could get her a gig writing for Vogue. Shaking in the glass-tipped snowflakes I was genuinely holding her sanity in question. There was no way she thought this was actually going to happen. But that's the thing about Mischa. Even when she knows better than to believe in something she lets it throw her a pitch anyway. She knows how to soften to the world, which is what you need if you want anything to reach you. She'll stand with both feet in the ocean and let herself get soaked to the knees or the neck depending on how high it feels like rising. For all the external back and forth, there is that stillness in her. *Chill out*, she said as I stomped out cigarette after cigarette to make a point of my rage. *You never know.*

You never know.

We filed into the bathroom as clandestinely as possible. Doing drugs, really doing anything in the bathrooms at Cubby is among the more challenging of nighttime hurdles. There are only two and both are cramped as hell and smell like a blend of vomit and discount cleaning fluid distilled over the years into a fine vapor, gently mixing with the synthetic royal pine spray emanating from diffusers above the sink. It is potentially the least attractive environment on the planet and no one goes in unless the situation is desperate. Obviously when you go in there with someone, everyone knows it's for one of two reasons, and if you're ambitious, both. Either way it's an enormous *fuck you* to the collective of rupturing bladders, which is enough to make you feel bad already, but if that hasn't given you sufficient anxiety, here you are trying to do blow with your best friend whose no-filter trust complex has the boundless capacity to get you both in trouble, and two strange girls with unclear emotional dynamics who could be proffering DMT or antifreeze for all you know at this point, and you're too drunk to know the difference, or care.

Mischa sucked up her bump first, then the model, whose name was Finn or Flynn – I couldn't remember so I decided it was Flynn – then the angry girl, and finally me. I dug the key into the corner of the bag. I was going last but I wasn't about to get shorted. I tried not to think about the terrible realities of the key, its wretched life spent shoved inside locks and noses and the bottoms of purses and dropped in the gutter, about how much is that what we get sick from, the poisonous things that sneak inside on the periphery. It's not the drugs that kill you it's the delivery. In middle school biology we learned that all smelling anything has to do with is tiny particles of the thing getting inside. All you need to do is drop your keys once on the sidewalk, and through no effort at all you've got a mainline of rat poison old blood bread crumbs and dog shit straight into the brain, and good luck trying to figure out what hurts. But it might be a measure of success, this. What exactly do you need to accomplish to have pure cocaine deposited into your head by a mini titanium spoon.

I held the little powder mountain up to my right nostril, clamped the left one shut with a stiff-knuckled finger and snorted. A crackle of electricity shot through my frontal lobe. My eyes watered. This wasn't standard issue New York City cocaine. The veins in my hands popped up a harsh violet blue. The filter got dialed up to SHARPEN. The dingy tones of the bathroom were suddenly awash in golden light and supersaturated with color, the dark stained walls and dirty floor tiles exploding in multifaceted browns and greens and reflective blacks. Mischa's hair, the coils of it, shiny black ringlets blip-scratching like record rings in my line of vision. I could feel the blood cells plush and zooming through their channels like inner tubes, individual atoms straining against their bonds. Holy shit.

All at once I became aware of the crazy pounding on the door – *GET THE FUCK OUT* – pound pound pound – which was so immediately terrifying that everything threatened to short-circuit. Without a word Flynn grabbed my hand to lead me out. Her head was balanced perfectly straight smack in the middle of her shoulders like a landmark, a Pythagorean structure whose angles and exactness took years to perfect and now because of its symmetry was among the wonders of the world. Walking out together we somehow avoided being harassed. Femme girls. They glide along the earth emanating holiness and untouchability, lipglossed and lingeried Jesuses in stilettos floating across the lake.

I could've been imagining it but if I wasn't before, the angry girl was certainly murdering me with her eyeballs now. The hand-grab was the final nail in the coffin. We walked to the bar, packed airtight with sweaty bodies. The chemical drip was making its slow descent, glopping down my throat like a giant squid through an elevator shaft. I swallowed repeatedly, licking an acrid saltiness off my lips as my heart thrummed in double bass. My tongue felt like it was tipped with pipe cleaner bristles. Mischa had negotiated the angry girl off to the jukebox, which was already in its fourth installment of Robyn. The entire bar, despite being full to capacity, was living its own sad girl narrative, dancing on its own.

"Do you want a drink?"

Flynn leaned down close to me. I loved her so much more in that moment than I'd ever loved anyone, for anticipating my desires before I could articulate them to myself.

"Vodka gimlet," I said. "Thank you."

The bartender came and a couple minutes later returned with the vodka and a cheap white wine for Flynn.

"So how long have you two been dating?"

I stared at her. For a minute I had no idea what she was talking about, until it dawned on me that she must be referring to Mischa.

"Misch?! Oh, we're not." Maybe I said that too quickly. "We're best friends. We do everything together. We're like Thelma and Louise."

I had no idea what Thelma and Louise had done because I'd never actually seen the movie, but people usually bring them up as a point of reference for best friendship so I went with it. It is my understanding that the whole thing centers on them attempting to escape some desperate circumstances, and at the end they go coasting off a cliff. This seems very noble. And accurate, as Mischa's the only person I would feel happy to die with. In my head I always describe us as Enid and Rebecca from *Ghost World,* because it's my favorite movie, but I feel like I should come up with a different example because the thought of us going down their road – one in khakis and a dead expression and one on a midnight bus to nowhere – fills me with fear.

"I could have sworn you guys were dating." Flynn took a long sip of her wine.

"Are you dating…?"

"Cass? I mean…"

I knew what that meant, it was written all over. Cass who couldn't believe her luck. Flynn who held her close and, being taller, investigated the rest of the room beyond her shoulder. Cass walking on the street side of the sidewalk with a swell of pride, Flynn who only held her hand in public when she was wasted. Who had a curated portfolio of words and Cass who absorbed them. After sex, a silence. I knew this scene. This scene didn't end well.

"Do you want to go outside?" She poured the rest of the wine in her mouth. "It's really hot in here. Let's have a cigarette."

We pushed through the crowd of bodies out the door. While in there the noise and the voices coalesced into one heavy hush, out here was nothing but dynamics. The entire world was sparking like a mad firework, stars burning holes in the soft black blanket that comprised the sky. They receded into the black and returned bright to their points, back and forth, Orion's belt oscillating like a sine wave. It blasted out in all directions but still somehow looked like a planetarium. Like a little box. Going about our activities, acting on acting like acting up inside the little box.

I felt arms around me. Sloan's arms heavy and charged with heat, mouth full of moonshine cherries. Leigh's thin and tentative, wrapping themselves around a force field inches from my skin. Nik's hard and self-assured, and Morgan's from a kinder world. And these, warm, smelling of cinnamon. The stars dropped down, one by one, into my eyes. Sloan and I in full ecstasy under the lights where she touched my skin and left her likeness, mouth open, mouth I could've swallowed, Flynn's mouth with its thin shellac of sugar scented balm, swallowing mine, becoming, aortal blood pound and warm liquid all over, a different siren hum in my skull. Light was flooding the world beneath my eyelids in wriggling spills of color against the black, blacker than black, supersaturated post-flashbulb black, so black it was white, first light seeping like honey into the blood and everything inside it, redness, blackness, dark blue, azure, pinpricks of stars on the insides of my eyes and the light reaching all the way up through, up cunt and cervix uterus organs up my throat out my mouth over eyelids to hold them shut and trap the universe inside – luminous blackness – the snap and the crush that sent my head reeling and sealed the image. The blood that ran down my philtrum was thick and sludgy, tasting of rusted metal and chemical powder, tightening against my mouth like an egg white mask.

Muzzy in the head on the subway, one of Mischa's hands clamped firmly over mine and the other trying internet searches for how to home-remedy a broken nose, it occurred to me that I had been punched in the face for the first time.

The air was not quite summer, not quite fall, cooled down from the heat that made the whole city feel like a bikram studio but still sticky, settling over the skin like cling film, carrying faint whiffs of salt and trash. Mischa and I walked through McCarren Park, sharing a water bottle of vodka soda with a squeezed out lime floating forlornly near the bottom. The soda had gone flat a while ago so now it tasted like something you'd use to sterilize a wound. We drank it anyway, not tasting, flushing it straight down to sanitize the bile.

"I love this park," Mischa said. "It's one of the only parks that still looks like a park."

That was true. The old Polish men still congregated here with their bathtub poison, dirty bottles of mud red wine, bundles of Żywiec cans strangled inside their plastic holders which, incidentally, were some of the most reasonably priced beers in the city, six dollars for four tall boys. It was one of the last places that felt like a real neighborhood, like people still lived here. Everything else seemed to have dissipated before we even showed up. I learned about what Tompkins Square Park was supposed to be from a photography book. Tompkins Square Park was already in the process of being sterilized when Mischa and I were being born. It was hard to picture the whitewashed, manicured enclosure as the scene of a riot, a small outdoor colony for the homeless and traveling and unlucky. The grainy black and white images had filled me with a sense of rootless longing. Not my specific loss, and yet.

There is a moment in the thick of loss, when you're really down in it, when it loses its tragic edge. Like a threshold of crush. Balance enough bad things on top and they start to flatten you, but throw a couple more on and you become buoyant. Elastic. It's strange. The burn hurts at first but hold the tip of the cigarette down a little longer and you begin to feel its warmth. Lose enough and there's less to carry. Dig down deep enough and you can't help but reach light: you've tunneled through the entire world.

Trzeba sobie jakoś radzić, powiedział baca, zawiązując buta dżdżownicą.

This doesn't translate well, but it's always been my mother's feel-better, and it's true –

You have to make it work somehow, said the mountain man, lacing up his boot with an earthworm.

"If we had a band, what would our name be?"

By now Mischa looked like a goddamn amateur painting, all white with two red splotches blooming across her sweaty cheeks. The cheeks were always a dead giveaway.

"What the fuck instruments do we know how to play? I can't even draw a guitar."

"I know, but if we had a band. If we could be like, I don't know, The Runaways. Or Hole. Like instead of trying to write anything or do anything we could just scream our message across the world and make people pay attention. Wouldn't that be cool?"

I nodded. I was still stuck on the insurmountable problem of not being able to play instruments. But on the other hand, lots of bands can't play instruments and they still come up with a following so maybe talent and ability don't have as much to do with success as image and drive. Don't fake it til you make it. Fake it til you've convinced yourself that you're real.

"Yeah, I guess it would be pretty cool."

We had collapsed on a bench by this point, narrowly missing a splatter of bird shit all over one side. The sun was there, thinking about whether to recede or not. Judging by our shadows it was about five in the afternoon.

There was a pair of drunk men installed on the bench across from ours, similarly red-faced but passed out on each other, the smaller one's head resting on the taller one's shoulder, the taller one's head balanced gently atop his friend's. They were breathing together in unison, chests rising and falling in slow, even cycles. They could've been a postcard. Greetings From The Edge Of The World. And I was so drunk that seeing two drunks passed out on a bench together was starting to move the heavy things inside me. My eyes misted over.

"What about, like, Poison Pussy? Like that woman who stuck a bunch of poison up her snatch because she wanted to kill her husband when he went down on her? That was sort of clever. But maybe not, it didn't work actually, he ended up taking her to the hospital because it started poisoning her instead, so that might be a reference to chivalry we don't want. Or maybe...I don't know...Fly Honey Warehouse? That has a snappy sort of ring to it. But I don't think it means anything…"

I nodded, watching the men. The taller one was snoring, droplets of drool falling like raindrops onto his friend's greasy head. Their boots were untied, filthy. Plaid workshirts, maybe from when they used to work, stained with sweat and spilled beer, darker where there was blood. They had gotten in a fight or two. Maybe once or twice with each other, but who remembered. Who cared. They breathed together in blessed sleep, holding each other up like two leaning towers forming one straight shot into the sky. The smaller one shifted and a traveling bottle of Sobieski crept out from within the folds of them. It fell to the ground with a soft clunk.

"Plastic Vodka Bottle Sleepover," I said, not taking my eyes off their movements.

Silence for a minute.

"What?" Mischa sat up with a shake. She had started drooping onto me as I sat transfixed by the men.

"The name. For our band. Plastic Vodka Bottle Sleepover. What do you think?"

She opened one eye at me, as if she were seeing me for the first time.

"That's the stupidest band name I've ever heard," she said, pasting herself back onto my arm and closing the eye imperially.

It's Christmas Eve, the Christmas we celebrate, twelve dishes laid out in honor of the twelve disciples. The window glass is latticed with ice that encroaches like ivy, building upon itself in intricate layers. Mom cheats every year, counting the bread and butter as a dish apiece.

Maybe housewives have the time to make twelve full dishes, she says. But I don't.

I don't remember who took this picture, all of us are in it. Our mother in her red silk blouse, the sharp points on either side of her more like hangers instead of shoulders, bifocals perched atop her nose. Grandma at the head of the table nodding off slightly – blackberry liqueur before dinner, she's 87 – regal in a gold knit cardigan and amber brooch, a furtive-looking insect trapped within. Atalanta in her cable-knit sweater with the thumbholes and worn jeans, smiling wide – the look on mom's face, Americans don't know how to dress for an occasion – you in even shittier jeans and an enormous black thermal, and me in the puff of blue tulle and rosettes I needled mom for. Two varieties of pickled herring, one with mushrooms and one with onions, sauerkraut with mushrooms and white beans, red beet soup – Ata couldn't say barszcz no matter what, I remember – uszka, the mushroom dumplings for that, also counting as a dish this year, the bread and the butter, and the pierogi, one kind with cheese and potato and the other with mushrooms. It looked like we also counted the salt, the pepper and the wine.

Ata's hand on your knee in the picture, your face open, smiling. Apparently she hated mushrooms, but she ate seconds of everything.

On New Year's Eve day I was hungover to the point of medical attention, all of my insides liquefied into one toxic stream, with the kind of urgency that makes you wish modern bathrooms came equipped with two toilets, one for under your ass and one for under your face, because at that point of sick you don't know whether you have the stronger need to shit or vomit and whichever you do first makes you feel like you should've done the other. Paper towels either way.

"We didn't even drink that much!" Sloan shouted through the door.

I responded with a wet heave loud enough to make her *ugh* in disgust. To Sloan, "didn't drink that much" meant we had made it home more or less safely, with most of our things still intact, cursing at each other only the normal amount. It said nothing about the actual volume of the drinking, or the horror level of the (cheap, likely poisonous) alcohol. Which is how we had started to gauge most situations, the degree to which we went off the rails. We drank "too much" Croatian moonshine the night she tried to tear out my nipple rings in an insane bout of paranoia about my future ability to breastfeed (Sloan wanted children), and "not that much" the night I walked home barefoot in the snow after throwing my heels in the street because my feet needed an immediate ice bath.

She knocked on the door again.

"Do you think you can at least pull it together by tonight?"

"If I can you'll be the first to know," I said into the toilet bowl, which echoed.

"Okay. Take a shower or something. I'm going to work." Another sigh. "And change the sheets."

Her voice receded, then her footsteps, the heavy hush after a door close and I was alone in the house.

Sloan didn't believe in hangovers. Which is sort of like saying she didn't believe in electrons or the rising sun, but there you go. When it came to that, or anything else that makes a person lie down, her go-to move was to deny deny because to admit to pain would amount to a personal shortcoming, because if you could still move your limbs and open your eyes you were responsible for the business of living, because only pathetic assholes attached the word "sick" to a self-imposed state. It was a tall order, and exhausting. My head sunk deeper into the toilet just thinking about it.

Even if I wanted to say no, and I did, I couldn't. We were supposed to be going to her parents' for New Year's Eve, the most important holiday. She'd done the coming out show with them and now that they had calmed down, they were curious to put a face to their daughter's most-spoken name. Unfortunately, my face was a mottled nightmare of white and green and red, blood-drained from nausea and dehydration except for the purpling broken vessels along my jaw and orbital bones. Sick, whether Sloan agreed with it or not. I rested my cheek on the cool seat.

In the basement we'd had a pre-New Year's celebration with the bartender who, over the months, had ended up with no choice but to become our friend as a result of our constant patronage. Sloan had moved into my apartment when we decided to get cohabitative, partly because it was bigger than her leaning attic and partly because of the bar underneath. The closest bar to her was blocks away, and with me being underage it was important to have a home base where we could drink in peace. Beyond that, the underground shithole was a special and holy place. We could unravel down there, close to the earth. No matter how loud it got, which overamped band was shaking debris off the ceiling or which enraged drunk was breaking bottles or noses, The Kiln retained a certain grounding silence. It was the one place that didn't exclusively belong to me or Sloan or the world, the first place we'd been face to face, the only place that was, in equal parts, ours.

We pushed open the metal door.

Will was bent over the bar, brow furrowed, examining his move against an invisible opponent. The three black pawns beside his right wrist had tipped over and were rolling lazily down the pockmarked wood, across from a formidable-looking pile of white pieces. He scowled at the board. Sloan plopped down on a stool.

"You're losing," she said. "Jesus, you're getting your ass kicked."

Will looked up at her.

"I know. My black half is better than my white. What'll it be tonight, ladies?"

"Let's start with water," Sloan said.

"Very good."

Will disappeared beneath the bar and produced an industrial-sized bottle of Kamchatka, the poor man's vodka's vodka, and poured it into two iced pint glasses, topping each off with a spritz of soda. He poured a glass for himself and we cheersed.

"New Year's plans?"

"Ah, yeah." That was me. "Big night tomorrow. Meeting the parents."

"A Robert de Niro New Year's, I love it! You should come down here when you're done. Or are you meeting the Fockers too?"

"Very funny. No, we're meeting her parents. I mean I'm meeting her parents. For the first time. She's already met them."

"Shit. Do they know about the…whole thing?" He looked at Sloan.

"You mean do they think we're just roommates? No, I told them what's going on."

"Well then you'd better be on your A game. Look nice, curtsy, no swearing and all that. Remember, you have to make up for the fact you're a girl."

"Oh come on. How bad can it go? Parents love me."

"Whose parents?"

"Mine tried."

"But you weren't fucking their daughter."

"We didn't talk about masturbation in my house."

"Oh my god."

"Come on, it's funny."

"Cinnamon Slut for good luck?"

"No," said Sloan.

"Yes!"

Sloan gave me a look.

"We shouldn't drink that much tonight."

I stared at her over the tower of Kamchatka.

"I'm saying we shouldn't drink much more."

"Not more. Just one."

"It's never just one."

"It's always just one."

"Cut up into pieces."

"I'm working on my portion control."

"You're going to be a mess tomorrow."

"I'm a mess right now."

Will shook his head, laughing.

Sometime around three a.m. we stumbled up the stairs, half-crawling, Sloan pulling me up by the arm every time I decided I wanted to sleep Right Here. When she opened the door to the room I collapsed on the covers, blissful and cool against my burning cheeks. I held them to my face and breathed in their air, sweat and smoke and some kind of flowers. The Cinnamon Sluts had worked us over. Will's specialty – a shot of Bailey's topped off with a shot of Goldschläger topped off with 151, then lit on fire and sprinkled with cinnamon to the effect of fireworks. The flames went up like a sparkler, shooting off toward the ceiling then vanishing into the ether mid-fall. You blew them out before the alcohol burned off and they were hot and sweet to drink, the burnt cinnamon crystallized into a thin crème brulée crust on the surface. You always asked for two or three more just to watch the flames.

"Baby." Sloan stretched out next to me. I felt her hand moving on me somewhere, hip or waist, I couldn't tell. "I love you."

"Mmmph."

"You know I love you, right?"

"Mmhm."

I knew I had the spins. I didn't want to open my eyes and confirm. I breathed steadily into the covers, trying to be as out of my body as possible. I always took myself here, to the edge I couldn't see over. I heard Sloan's voice echo in the distance somewhere, the word "love" every so often. If she was talking about love that meant she wasn't upset. That was good. That meant I hadn't said anything stupid and we wouldn't have to have a fight, and I could sleep. I breathed deeper into the folds.

The hand moved.

"I'm serious. I've been with people I loved before, and thought it was real, and maybe it was, I don't know. But I was young, and you know…you know how they say you're always looking for that other thing, the thing that speeds your blood. I think you might be it for me. You."

Light pressure, button snap, zipper. The stir of the air against something warm.

"You're the last thing I ever wanted. And now I can't want anything else."

I realized I had to piss terribly. I also knew if I opened my mouth I would vomit. She nudged me over to give herself a better angle and when she did all the liquid collected inside of me went sloshing around like suds in a basin. I squeezed my legs together and focused on my breath, thinking of heat.

"But sometimes it's strange. You lead me in to a point and then disappear."

Heat, heat and drought, dull dehydration headache.

"I can be looking at you and touching you and one minute you're there and then you're not. Even your skin feels different. It's like your blood stops moving."

"You're going to think this is crazy, but sometimes I forget what you look like. Like I know I'd recognize you in a picture or something, but I can't remember your face when you're not there."

Heat rising in S-curves, white light on the asphalt.

"Where do you go when you're not there?"

The sun in my eyes.

"Jesus fucking Christ!"

The water that spilled over me was smooth and warm like butter and went instantly freezing, my stomach concave with the steep decompression. I heard Sloan's voice go up through the dead dark across the walls and the ceiling before spiraling down into door slam darkness, drowned out eventually by a rush of water in the far off toilet. I walked close to the mist from the sprinklers as I went on bare feet down the driveway, past the kids picking scabs off their knees. Through the lot with the weeds in the asphalt, by the shop where I bought my first menthols, to the place where you sat by the river, in the place where I got my first burn.

My arms are wrapped around your neck in the picture, calf muscles pulled tight beneath the enormous Pink Floyd shirt I'm swimming in as I stand on tiptoe to reach you. The pivonias are overripe, shot through with crimson veins, their scent heavy and poison-sweet rising from petals crushed into the damp cement. The U-Haul is in the driveway, packed and waiting. Your life is starting over.

I clung on longer than a hug is supposed to last, trying to squeeze a lifetime of memory into those last few seconds. You tousled my hair, freeing a handful of dirty blonde wisps from the half-assed braid mom threw together that morning. You gave my shoulders a tight little squeeze.

Trzymaj się, siostra.

Hold onto yourself.

You drove away before you got a chance to give me your expert advice on starting first grade.

Nareszcie, mom said as the truck disappeared around the corner. Finally. We can do something about the mess in that room.

These are the other things you left for me:

1) The pyramid of Coke cans. I wasn't alive for the actual thing but there's a picture from before I was born, you in these bright blue shorts, so blue they made your eyes hurt, and tiny – Slavic people and their tiny shorts, the childhood rite of passage – smiling from one side of the frame to the other because you'd built something bigger than you were, even at the risk of giving yourself diabetes. According to our mother you gained fifteen pounds that summer, but made it a point to tell everyone you drained each of the cans yourself.

2) The iron cross necklace, which I stole and wore for the first grade yearbook photo, completely out of place among the Lisa Frank and cheetah print but with all the giddy pride of wearing a really cool thing that couldn't possibly be mine. Was only moderately hurt later on when you pointed out the picture recalled a smaller, chubbier Glenn Danzig.

3) A Marlboro in a half-crushed pack, flipped upside down.

4) The vinyl.

Something else about airports: the bathroom mirrors will make you think about buying a coffin, if you weren't thinking about it already. I'm always surprised whenever I look in a mirror, because I'm constantly forgetting what I look like, but this one is really something. This time I look like the inside. Dead upon waking. Dead and awake.

Going nowhere. Writing letters.

I can still feel the window glass against my forehead where I was leaning on it, the chill trapped beneath my skin. The smell of sweat and convenience food and travel. Disturbance and change. The feeling that something's about to HAPPEN. Pensive piano. Magical unrest.

This hand dryer unrelenting. The whirr replacing my brain beat.

On my first day here I went to the Barnes & Noble in Union Square, that tells you how well I knew my way around, I'll never go back. There was a red haired kid, red like firetruck not red like natural orange, who I first saw outside before he got the horrors. I had forgotten about him until later, when I looked up from *The Book of Hours* to see him getting carried out, one cop at his feet and another at his shoulders, bloodrushed in the face screaming incomprehensible crazy in this desperate primal pitch that collapsed the veins. On their way out I caught his eye, blue like flame center, blue like that pool of water in the abandoned paper mill in Sagamore Hills, and even though the self I was that day was a self I barely remember, to this day I could identify that exact piercing shade of blue.

Small things.

There's a scar on my cheek where I cut my own face. I told you it was from the cat when you asked me. That's another thing I lied to you about. It was right after and it was winter. The snow on the ground was thick like sugar, like powder, something sweet and warm, and I wasn't sure how to tell you there was no violence in it, I just needed to make sure I still inhabited myself.

I'm thinking about that movie where the guy starts living in an airport because it's the only place he can stay indefinitely.

I'm not a hundred percent sure you liked Courtney Love. I don't think we ever talked about it. I know you liked Nirvana. You didn't think Kurt was a god in human form, though, even though you understood his genius. You never crossed the line into blind, uncritical love of anything. You never thought any one thing was The Best Thing. It's not like you ever told me that to my face, I could just tell, the way a person intuits a tendency. The way I knew you thought taking coffee non-black was ridiculous, even though you didn't say it. If you're going to do something just do the fucking thing was your attitude, toward coffee and everything else. You always knew better than to put all your trust in one place.

You were born with the things most people spend a lifetime discovering.

Still, I want to tell you about the time I met Courtney Love. I think maybe you would have thought it was funny. She walked into the sex shop and threw a cock ring on the floor. It vibrated sadly on the tiles. She laughed for a bit and then left. It wasn't quite the celebrity encounter I had in mind but then again, don't we always end up disillusioned by the people we really idolize?

I've spent a quarter life wondering who you are.

Acknowledgments

Thank you, first and foremost, to Amanda Miska, my publisher and sister art monster, for bringing this book into the world. To my parents, for their continuous support, and to Uncle Bill for keeping my head up.

Enormous thanks to Darcey Steinke, my fantastic teacher and friend, without whom this book would not exist. To Elizabeth Benson-Colligan, Lee K. Abbott, Shelley Jackson, Patrick McGrath, Frederic Tuten, Debra Moddelmog and Sebastian D.G. Knowles – I am endlessly grateful for your guidance and encouragement. Thank you Michelle Tea for being a constant inspiration.

Thank you to thesis nuts James Hargrave, Tom Barranca and Brandon Weavil. To Mike DeSanti, whom this book is for – thank you for your supreme eyesight and firm grip on things. Thank you to Christopher Hermelin, Jonah Fried, Marianne McKey and Rachel Broderick, for your loving reads and invaluable criticism. To the rest of my New School family: I am lucky to know you.

Kristen Smith, Lindsay Hearts, Jamie Reich, Kati Massaro, Cori Zanin and Alexa Pokorny – thank you for your endless love. To my drDOCTOR family, Sam Farahmand and Luke Wiget, thank you for keeping me awake. To editors Stephanie Georgopulos, Jac Jemc, Joe O'Brien, Laia Garcia, Ian Kappos, Jason Buhrmester, Kyle Lucia Wu, Tobias Carroll, and Gwen Werner – thank you for seeing something in me.

To everyone who has helped me out over the years, who has given me coffee, kind words, a place to stay, a laptop, a job to support myself in the making of this novel, and countless other things: Stef Schwartz, Craig Mathis, Lisa Rosa, Saeed Jones, Laura Jayne Martin, Elyssa Goodman, David Moore, Brandon Bartling, Jenny Mae Clark and many others, thank you from the bottom of my heart.

Thank you Mars for going up in flames with me. Thank you Silas for saving my life. And thank you Jeff, my love, for holding on to me always.

*

Parts of this novel have appeared in *Joyland*, *Vol.1 Brooklyn*, and *Luna Luna Magazine*.

Reading List

The Diving Bell and the Butterfly, Jean-Dominique Bauby

Hopscotch, Julio Cortázar

Garden State, Rick Moody

Venus in Furs, Leopold von Sacher-Masoch

Justine, Philosophy in the Bedroom, and Other Writings, Marquis de Sade

Bohemian Manifesto: A Field Guide to Living on the Edge, Laren Stover

The Story of O, Pauline Réage

Childe Harold's Pilgrimage, Lord Byron

Nausea, Jean-Paul Sartre

Groundwork of the Metaphysics of Morals, Immanuel Kant

Just Kids, Patti Smith

Plutonian Ode and Other Poems, Allen Ginsberg

The Happy Birthday of Death, Gregory Corso

Desolation Angels, Jack Kerouac

Dirty Hits: Stories 2003-2013, Tony O'Neill

Junky, William S. Burroughs

More, Now, Again: A Memoir of Addiction, Elizabeth Wurtzel

Carrie's Story, Molly Weatherfield

The Good Soldier Švejk, Jaroslav Hašek

Valencia, Michelle Tea

Beautiful Wreck: Sex, Lies & Suicide, Stephanie Schroeder

An Enquiry Concerning Human Understanding, David Hume

Ghost World, Daniel Clowes

Tompkins Square Park, Q. Sakamaki

The Book of Hours, Rainer Maria Rilke

*

The lines "Humping the American Dream" and "Bad craziness" are taken from *Fear and Loathing in Las Vegas* by Hunter S. Thompson.

Playlist

"Box of Rain" – Grateful Dead, *American Beauty*

"Comfortably Numb" – Pink Floyd, *The Wall*

"My Blakean Year" – Patti Smith, *trampin'*

"Smile?" – The Crystal Method, *Divided By Night*

"Straight To Video" – Mindless Self Indulgence, *You'll Rebel To Anything*

"Skinny Little Bitch" – Hole, *Nobody's Daughter*

"Dream Brother" – Jeff Buckley, *Grace*

"Don't Take Your Love Away From Me" – Neil Young, *Lucky Thirteen*

"People Are Strange" – The Doors, *Strange Days*

"I Wanna Dance With Somebody" – Whitney Houston, *Whitney*

"San Francisco" – Foxygen, *We Are the 21st Century Ambassadors of Peace & Magic*

"Autumn Leaves" – Bob Dylan, *Shadows in the Night*

"Graveyard" – Feist, *Metals*

"I'd Rather Be High" – David Bowie, *The Next Day*

"Phantasmagoria in Two" – Tim Buckley, *Goodbye and Hello*

"Know Your Rights" – The Clash, *Combat Rock*

"Dancing On My Own" – Robyn, *Body Talk*

"You Drive Me Wild" – The Runaways, *The Runaways*

"Dumb" – Nirvana, *In Utero*

"Hold On To Me" – Courtney Love, *America's Sweetheart*

*

Available on Split Lip's Spotify. **Username**: split_lip

About the Author

Mila Jaroniec earned her MFA in fiction from The New School. She is the editor of drDOCTOR and her work has appeared in *Playboy, Hobart, Vol. 1 Brooklyn, LENNY, Joyland* and *Teen Vogue*, among others. *Plastic Vodka Bottle Sleepover* is her first novel.

AND DISCOVER MORE IN

Great literature and music, brought to you monthly.

WEBSITE: www.splitlipmagazine.com
FACEBOOK: facebook.com/splitlipmagazine
TWITTER: @splitlippress

Made in the USA
Charleston, SC
02 November 2016